Also by PAUL WILLCOTT

Annals of Franklin Manor
A Franklin Manor Christmas
A Franklin Manor Epiphany

Standalone
12,000 Miles of Road Thoughts. Old Van, Old Man, Recovering
Hippie, Dying Cat

Watch for more at paulwillcott.com.

A Franklin Manor Epiphany

By

Paul Willcott

Illustrations by

Walle Conoly

Annals of Franklin Manor

Book Two

A FRANKLIN MANOR EPIPHANY

First edition. July 29, 2022.

ISBN: 979-8223266082

Written by PAUL WILLCOTT.

FOR THE RESIDENT ANGELS OF FRANKLIN
MANOR

Chapter One
A Visitor

They had just finished breakfast in the basement dining room, which the nuns had called the refectory. They didn't linger at the table. All four of them felt some urgency to wash the dishes and set the room to rights and get on with things. Never mind that none of them had anything to get on with.

Nurse and Scap, both in their eighties, should have felt free to drink coffee and chat and do little for as long as they wanted. Jane Felsher Kravitz was more than two generations younger, but she'd been pretty well banged up when a car hit her two days earlier. Still, she was the first one to push her chair back and start clearing away. Former Professor Regent had nothing on his agenda, and his muscles were tight and achy from working on the old house and sledding with some kids, so he should have been happy to be idle. But Regent was restless by nature.

That it was a Saturday and the day after Christmas and they'd been through a lot recently made no difference. They all felt like they should be getting on with something. Anything.

When they finished cleaning up, they made their way up to the ground-floor parlor of the cavernous Victorian house and put another log on the fire and riffled through all eight pages of the Oliver's Mountain *Eagle* for stories they might have overlooked the first time through.

"Well, at least it's not snowing anymore," Scap said. His thin, old man's voice belied his vigor. "Could do with a little sunshine, though."

Nurse gave a polite little grunt of affirmation. Jane nodded agreement.

Former Professor Regent made no response at all. He was standing with his back to the fire and looking out the bow windows that opened onto the sweeping front porch. It was a gray, cheerless day, as Scap had pointed out, but the cloud cover kept the temperature in the high teens. That was a relief after the extreme cold of the past week.

At that moment, a man emerged from behind the cedar trees at the bottom of the sloping front yard. He advanced a couple steps up the driveway, then stopped and stared fixedly at the house.

If he was looking for an address, that would be unusual. Everyone in Oliver's Mountain and for miles around knew Franklin Manor.

When Regent had bought it several years earlier, it didn't even have a number posted. And he'd not put one up.

The man out front must be from away.

After studying the house for a while, he trudged up through the deep snow of the unplowed driveway. He wore a fur cap with the flaps tied under his chin, a puffy, Michelin-man type parka, which was soiled and worn, and down mittens. He had a scarf across his face. Yep, clearly not a local. It was just not that cold.

"You know," Jane said, "under all those clothes that could be almost any person of medium height. From the way of walking, I'd say he's a man, but it's hard to be certain about even that little bit."

Jane was a writer, at least she had wanted to be a writer when she'd been Professor Regent's student some years earlier. Since Regent's chance encounter with her on Christmas Eve when she'd had her accident, he'd not asked her what she was doing these days. In any case, she was still a careful observer.

Regent went to the door. "Hello," he said. "May I help you?"

The stranger pulled back his scarf revealing a pink, wind-chapped face. He had some wrinkles, but for some reason, they seemed to have arrived ahead of schedule. A wisp of blond hair hung from under his fur cap. He had a straight, sharp nose and eyes as blue as the Adirondack sky on a clear day.

"Would you be Butch Regent, like on the mailbox?" he asked. The man's speech was all magnolias and corn pone. Maybe that was why he was wearing too many clothes.

Regent's good manners kept him from saying what first came to his English-professor mind. "Do you mean 'would I be Butch Regent, *if I could*?'" Quite different from, "Are you Butch Regent?".

"I am. What can I do for you?"

"My name is Dick Chandler. I'm a writer, and I'm working on a story. Can I ask you some questions? Sorry if I'm intruding."

Oh, one of those, Regent thought. So many stories have been published about this old house, they're almost a cliché. Still, he'd give the man a few minutes. There was nothing else going on.

"Come in," he said.

They went into the parlor, and Regent introduced him to the others.

"This is Delia Broussard, Jane Felsher Kravitz, and Jason Goehring."

"Scap," Goehring corrected.

"Scap?" Chandler asked.

"Yeah. Short for scapular."

Chandler stretched his neck up in an effort to peer over Scap's shoulder. "I've never known anyone named for the shoulder blade," he drawled. His expression was so blank it was not possible to tell if he was teasing.

Scap decided the man was serious. "Not that. It's for the small medallions of the Virgin that you wear on a necklace. I used to award them to people."

"Why'd you do that?" he asked. "That" had two almost two complete syllables.

"It was a reward for helping the nuns when this house was a monastery." The pitch of his voice rose a little in irritation.

"Nuns? Don't you mean 'convent'?"

The old man sighed. "You must be a Protestant. You don't have to be a monk to live in a monastery. Convents are for working nuns. Teachers and the like. Our ladies spent their time in prayer and meditation. They were cloistered until Vatican II. Never went out. Even had a dentist's office in the back. So this place where they lived was a monastery."

"Oh." Chandler's blank expression remained unchanged.

"Also, Delia is called Nurse. That's what she was for as far back as most people remember."

"Nice to meet y'all." Still no expression.

"What're you working on?" Regent asked.

"I'm not sure." Chandler held up a small tape recorder. "Do you mind?"

"I don't suppose so," Regent answered.

"How about y'all?" Chandler asked the others.

They didn't object.

"How long have y'all lived in Oliver's Mountain?"

Regent answered. "I've been here several years. Scap and Nurse, most of their lives."

"How about you, Jane?" Chandler asked.

"Not long," she said, half smiling.

"What's it like living in this village?"

"I suppose about like living anywhere else," Regent answered. "What do you think, Scap?"

"Probably is."

Nurse smiled and nodded in agreement.

"But I wouldn't really know," Scap added. "I've never lived anywhere else. Hardly even been anywhere else."

"Anything unusual happen here lately?" Chandler asked.

Regent thought about the past few days. A hint of a smile crossed his face. Nurse and Scap looked at each other.

He could have told Chandler about strangers arriving to repair his plumbing at no cost and then coming again to keep the house from freezing up when the power went off and then others surprising them with Christmas dinner and firewood and Scotch whisky. He could have told Chandler about those unusual things and more. But he didn't.

If he had, Nurse and Scap would have said these occurrences were not unusual. In their view, even Liam's Christmas Eve appearance in the living room – Liam, who had been dead for years – was not unusual. Regent didn't want to have that discussion – not with this man he didn't know.

"No, not really," he said to Chandler.

"What are you working on, Mr. Chandler?" Regent asked again.

"Call me Dick." He took in a breath like a swimmer about to attempt a deep dive. "Can we just, you know, talk?"

Regent poked at the fire and moved the logs around.

"Where would you like to start?"

"I'm not sure," he drawled.

After a fairly long silence, Jane went smart mouthed. "Is it bigger than a breadbox?"

Chandler didn't seem to register her tone. After another period of silence, he said, "This is quite a house. Big. Old."

Jane and Regent exchanged glances.

Hoping the fellow was not going to be too, too strange, Regent politely gave him a little background. When he had bought it a few years ago, it had been a monastery for a long time. For decades before that, it was Franklin Manor Sanatorium, one of the area's many cure cottages.

"Cure cottages?"

"Yeah. Residences that were adapted to care for TB patients by exposing them to fresh air on open porches, waking and sleeping, all year around, no matter how cold."

"Delia was a nurse here for many years." He could have added, "a beloved nurse, borderline legendary."

"You live in this big place alone, Professor?"

It was a simple yes/no question, but it caused Regent to revert to his professor self. He looked at a spot about three quarters of the way up the wall, knitted his brow, half closed his eyes, and fell into serious deliberation. Finally arriving at precisely the correct formulation, he said, "Generally speaking, I do."

"Y'all just came over for breakfast?" Chandler asked the others.

"They're staying with me for a while," Regent said.

"Oh."

"Y'all are all old friends, huh?"

"Not exactly."

Regent didn't want to tell the man that he'd known Nurse for only a few days but that he was in the process of becoming her guardian and that he'd known Scap for less time than that, but that he had moved in yesterday – temporarily, of course – or that he hadn't seen Jane in some years, until he'd run into her, apparently homeless, the day before yesterday – Christmas Eve. The fellow didn't need to know all that. And besides, the telling would call it all to his own attention. He didn't want that either.

"What brings you to Franklin Manor, Dick?" Regent asked.

"Oh, well, I was walking by, and I saw the house. It seemed like a good place to start."

They waited for him to continue.

When he didn't, Jane asked, "So Dick, what brought you to Oliver's Mountain instead of to, say, Pittsburgh?"

"Oh. I see what you mean. I was memorizing names of counties, and as I was working my way through New York State, I happened to see Oliver's Mountain on the map. Then I had a dream in which I was instructed to come here." His face remained expressionless.

"I'll be going now. Nice to visit with y'all."

Before anyone could figure out how to respond, he'd put on his heavy clothes and was struggling down the snowy driveway.

Chapter Two
Herman Melville Meets Glenn Miller

"In this house, every day's an adventure," Regent said, shaking his head.

"Do you get a lot of that sort of thing?" Jane asked.

"It depends on what you mean by 'that sort of thing,'" Regent answered. "Maybe this one's merely eccentric. Not like Liam." *Oops.* He hadn't meant to bring that up.

"Who's Liam?" Jane asked.

Regent answered quickly before Scap or Nurse could say anything. "Oh, just another peculiar visitor who showed up here the other day."

Since yesterday afternoon, when they'd finished the big Christmas dinner that Sister Julia had surprised them with, life had begun to be more ordinary. He wanted to keep it that way.

"I'm going to my room and read," Regent said. "There are playing cards in that drawer" – he pointed to a table – "and obviously lots of books."

Partway up the stairs, he turned around and said, "If anyone else knocks on the door, don't answer it." It didn't come out as funny as he had intended.

He lowered himself heavily into the stuffing-leaking leather chair in front of the big window and gazed out at the village and the lake and beyond both, the mountain for which the village was named.

He'd brought up *Moby Dick*, *A Passage to India*, *Heart of Darkness*, a collection of Thoreau's essays, and an old *Atlantic Monthly* he'd found in a neighbor's recycling bin.

Given the dawdling, word-caressing way he read, that was enough material to last for months. He knew that. But it was like setting out on a mountain hike, even a short one in familiar territory; always a good idea to have emergency gear and extra food. What if he'd brought only *Moby Dick* (which he hadn't looked at in years), and then, for some reason, he hadn't found it engaging? He'd have to go back downstairs and get a different book. Nothing wrong with that. Except it would mean contact with the others, and he wanted some time alone.

Maybe he should have been more careful what he'd wished for in his early days in Franklin Manor. Actually, it had been more than a mere wish.

In the beginning, he hadn't known why he'd bought the house – it was as if he'd been compelled to – but he'd hardly begun the renovation, when, like a sudden mountain storm, the dream formed itself. He would turn the house into an artists' colony or retreat center, a sort of minor version of Yaddo in Saratoga Springs.

As strong as the urge was, he had never set out in detail, even to himself, what he had in mind. He never got much beyond happy visions of the house being full of people who were good at conversation (an uncommon gift in Regent's view), who appreciated books and music, who were kind and generous. Everything else would follow.

When he'd gone broke and had to stop work on the house before more than a small part of it had been renovated, he put the dream away.

But downstairs in the parlor at this very moment were three people who constituted a start – of sorts – on the community he'd envisioned. They weren't especially accomplished or artistic, but they were good people, interesting people. They'd do just fine for a start.

Something was seriously wrong with the picture, though. He had so little income, that even the small increase in utility bills caused by their presence was a problem.

He opened *Moby Dick* and began to read. He needn't have brought so many books up. This one engaged him immediately.

In the middle of Chapter 2, in the frosty street outside the Spouter-Inn – *had Melville himself inserted that wayward hyphen?* – Ishmael was suddenly joined by the Glenn Miller band. Regent loved Glenn Miller. Indeed, it was his own scratchy old LP someone was playing. But he didn't want to hear it now. He wanted to read about the whale. There was a time to read and a time to listen to music, and they must never be allowed to occur simultaneously. It was one of *Regent's Rules*.

Another person might have simply asked the guests to turn it off and thought no more about it. To Regent that seemed ungenerous. But when *Moonlight Serenade* ended and *Pennsylvania 6-5000* began, he closed the book on his index finger and went downstairs.

Jane was sitting on the floor surrounded by his collection of old records, reading album notes, humming, her head bobbing.

She didn't hear him come in.

"Jane," he said loudly, "Your timing is off." He didn't say the rest of what he felt – that he didn't like her going through his collection.

"What? Oh. No problem." She smiled and lifted the needle.

"Thank you," he said.

"No problem," she said again.

He went back upstairs, clutching Melville tightly to his chest. In his chair again, he opened the book to where he'd left off, and let circulation return to his finger. It was no good. He couldn't get back into it.

He'd gotten what he wanted. She'd turned off the music, and the house was quiet again. So, what was the problem? For one thing, her saying "no problem" was the problem. It was tied with "whatever" at the top of a list of expressions he didn't like. It was especially irritating when spoken by an adult.

But mostly it was about her getting into his record collection without asking. She could have picked up any book without it bothering him, but the records were different. He'd collected them over many years. Some were irreplaceable. He kept them in a special cabinet and organized them on a timeline according to when he'd obtained them. They were "his" in a way few things were. Not that he didn't like to share them. It was always a pleasure to play them for friends and talk about them one by one. He would have enjoyed having that dance with

Jane, but now he could not, not in the full, commanding way he would have liked.

Chapter Three
Chandler Sees Something

Regent went down to the kitchen at midday, made a turkey sandwich, and took it back to his room. He ate it slowly and stared out the big front window. The scene before him was all gray indolence. He gave in to it without resistance and spent the afternoon napping and reading and enjoying being alone.

By the time the sun made its early winter departure, he felt more sociable. Maybe they could all enjoy a drink together. There was still some of that Christmas gift of very fine Scotch whisky.

In the parlor, Scap had coaxed an enthusiastic blaze from the logs that had been quietly smoldering through the early afternoon. Nurse was pouring tea.

"Hello, Professor," she said. "I made a pot of tea. Would you like a cup"

"Thank you, Nurse, but I was thinking of something stronger."

In the makeshift bar he'd set up in the monastery's sacristy, he poured three fingers of whisky, no ice. Partway to the parlor, he went back for the bottle.

"Would you two like some of this?"

"Is the Pope Catholic?" Scap said.

"Nurse?"

"Yes, please. A little in my tea."

Scap sat down and took a sip and pronounced life good.

Regent agreed, but less wholeheartedly than Scap.

Abruptly, he said, "Scap, you can sit in any chair in this room, except the one you're in now." It was another of *Regent's Rules*. He smiled and softened his tone a little. "I guess you didn't see the sign. Sometimes it's invisible."

Scap looked around, frowning in confusion.

"It's on the seat," Regent said. "Still can't see it? I guess you have to have special eyes. It says, 'Professor Butch Regent's Personal Chair.'"

Scap stood up and looked at it. "Oh yeah. There it is," he said cheerfully. "Don't know how I missed it."

Regent was glad Scap was smiling.

Scap bit into a crisp cookie, broadcasting a shower of crumbs over a wide area.

"You should try one of these peanut butter cookies Nurse made, Professor."

Inwardly, Regent winced. Just when he'd quite masterfully solved the chair conflict, the old man had to make a mess. Not only that, he'd said "you should," another formulation he could not abide. Why couldn't Scap have said, "These cookies are delicious," or "I recommend these cookies?"

He let it go. "Where's Jane?"

"Gone to the grocery store. She was feeling better and wanted to get out of the house for a bit," Nurse answered. "I thought – if it's OK with you – we'd have leftovers for dinner, but we needed milk and a few things."

"Sounds good. Well, shall we watch the news?" Without waiting for an answer, he turned on the television.

When it was over, Nurse went to the kitchen and put out dinner. At 7:00, Jane had still not returned.

"Let's make do with what we have and not wait for Jane," Regent said. "I'm hungry."

They were midway through the meal when she arrived. Chandler was with her.

"Hi. I ran into Dick in the grocery store, and I invited him to join us for dinner."

Regent smiled and pointed to a chair. For the remainder of the meal, he was occupied with thoughts of how quickly things change. Only a few days ago, he would have been eating alone. Probably having sardines and canned beans. It was nice to have company. Not absolutely nice. Not simply nice. And Jane was pushing the envelope to ask people to dinner the way she had. Still – nice.

"I'm making progress on my story," Dick drawled.

"Oh. Does that mean you've found a subject?" Regent asked. He immediately regretted his sarcasm.

If Chandler was bothered, he didn't show it.

"Would you pass the mashed potatoes, please. I'm very hungry," Chandler said.

"I saw something really interesting in the grocery store." He slowed his chewing and seemed to lose track of what he was saying.

"Tell them, Dick," Jane prompted.

He shook his head briefly as if to clear it, reached into his backpack,, and pulled out a couple of pages. "I stopped at the library and used its computer to write a draft. I'll just read it to you."

Regent had mixed feelings. He'd had a lot of those lately. If the guy was accomplished, this little performance could be OK. On the other hand, he didn't want people to come in out of the cold – at someone else's invitation, yet – and take over his dining room.

"Hold on a minute, Dick," Jane said. She went into the kitchen and got the coffee pot and a plate of Nurse's cookies. She sat down again and said, "OK, go."

Chandler began reading.

It was getting dark. The parking lot and sidewalks were covered with worn two-day old snow.

At the supermarket, I noticed a couple who were probably shy of twenty. Their clothes were dirty, and they had studs and rings stuck into various parts of their heads. He had a tattoo on his neck that said, 'Hers.' She had one on her neck that said, 'His.'

They seemed poor, but they had each other, and they stopped now and then to kiss and carry on the way young lovers do.

I lost track of them for a while, but then I spotted them in the checkout line. They were at the counter emptying their pockets looking for more money. They had maybe a dozen items – just a few things for the kind of supper that housekeeping teenagers would want on a Saturday night. Macaroni, chips, cheese, soda – I've forgotten what all.

When they realized they didn't have enough money, the girl started putting things back.

"How much do you have?" the checker asked.

They kept emptying their pockets. They were short a little over three dollars.

The checker reached into her own pocket and handed them what she found there – two singles.

The gangly young bag boy offered up the few coins he had – it was still not enough – then hurried off in the direction of the stock room.

"We'll just put some things back," the couple said almost in unison as they tried to calculate costs and just get through the experience without too much discomfort.

The bag boy reappeared with money he'd collected in the stockroom.

But by then, it was too late and too hard. The young couple had gotten embarrassed and proud. They pushed a bag of Oreos and a few other things to one side, paid what they could, and left. It was awkward. It was wonderful.

"That's all I have," Chandler said. "So, what about it?"

Each waited for someone else to speak.

Jane gave Regent a look that warned him against an English-prof type critique. She herself made do with, "It's interesting, Dick." He didn't seem to want more than that.

"Here's what I want to know," he said. "Do things like that happen a lot around here?"

Nurse responded matter-of-factly. "Certainly."

Scap agreed.

"What if acts of kindness *are* common here?" Regent asked. "Is it your view, Dick, that Oliver's Mountain is unique in that way?"

"That, Professor, is the question," Chandler said. "I had a dream that directed me to come here and look for something. Maybe that's it."

"Maybe what's it?" Regent asked.

"To see if this is a place where people treat each other in a special way."

"Yes, well, people here are quite kind and generous, especially at this time of year," Nurse said. "But kindness and generosity exist everywhere."

"Uh huh. Anyway, I'll keep on observing," Chandler said. "I sure thank y'all for supper. Good night now."

He put on his Michelin-man parka, fur hat, and down mittens, went upstairs, and let himself out.

As they were washing dishes, the doorbell rang. It was Chandler.

"Did you forget something?" Regent asked.

"No, I don't think so." He patted himself down to be sure. "I was wondering. Could I take a bath before I go, Professor?"

Regent couldn't think of a reason to say no.

He was in bed with the great white whale, when he heard the water stop running.

Chapter Four
Noises in the Night

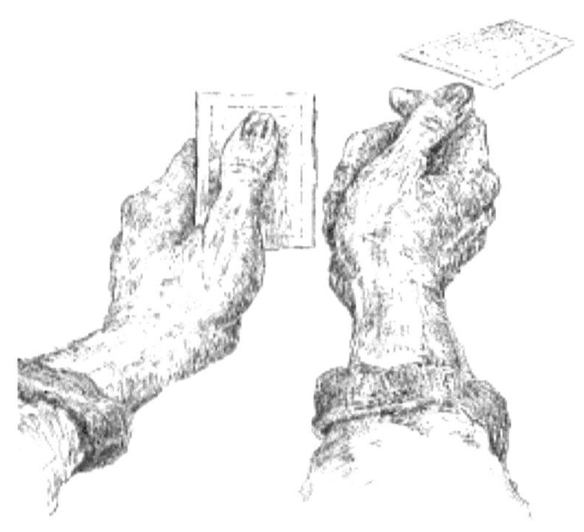

During the night, Regent woke up wanting a turkey sandwich and a little cranberry sauce and maybe some warmed-over dressing. It had been a long time since he'd had a fridge full of holiday leftovers.

He made his way toward the basement without turning on lights. He never turned on lights unless he had to. It cost too much.

When he had retired for the night, stepped onto the freezing cure porch off his bedroom, slipped into his mummy bag, and honored the departed Maalox with an imaginary pat on the head, a windy cold front had begun whistling in from Lake Ontario. As he went downstairs, the front was breaking up the cloud cover, and the light of a full moon flashed through ever-shifting openings. It flickered through the big windows, creating a strobe effect, now fleeting, now languorous, all around the old house.

As he reached the first floor, he heard noises coming from somewhere in the back of the house.

He opened a door and peered into a sort of storeroom just as a cloud obscured the moon, and everything went dark. But he knew the room well. The nuns had used it for sewing and handicrafts. Now it was cluttered with paint cans and plywood and two sawhorses.

Stepping around some buckets, his foot struck something he hadn't expected – something soft – something that recoiled from his contact – and he fell. As he hit the floor, moonlight came streaming through the window again. Sitting with her legs stretched out in front of her, was Jane.

She held her finger to her lips. Alarmed as he was, he didn't cry out.

"Are you all right?" he mouthed.

"I'm fine. You?" she whispered.

He nodded.

"What are you doing, Jane?" He left out the obscenities he would have liked to use. They would have been inappropriate, given the professor-student decorum they were still operating under.

They remained silent for a moment during which she cocked her head in listening posture and held up an index finger to ask for time and quiet. When no more of the sound she was listening for came, she stood up and turned on the light.

"I guess that's it for now," she said. "Professor, I'm hungry. Let's go to the kitchen, and I'll tell you about it."

"Sounds good to me," Regent said. "We've got Durkee. Just the thing for a turkey sandwich. You like Durkee? "

"Do I like Durkee?" she said, rolling her eyes. "Who do you think bought it?"

"Oh. Good move." He started pulling things from the fridge. "What's going on Jane?"

"Something woke me. It sounded like people talking and walking around."

Regent liked Jane, and he wanted her not to be a problem. What he did want was to have a sandwich and a glass of milk, go back to bed, and have this not be happening. But he was into it now.

"And?" he prodded halfheartedly.

"And I followed the sound from room to room. It seemed to come from one of those unused rooms at the back. It was intermittent, though – sometimes long periods of quiet – so I couldn't be sure exactly where. By the way, why did you buy such an enormous house, anyway?" She went on without waiting for an answer. "There was something really odd about it. I wasn't afraid, of course – you know me – but I still didn't want to go room by room opening doors."

Involuntarily, his eyebrows went up in a way that urged her to go on.

"I had the sense that – well – I'd be intruding. Like I said, it was odd. So, I sat on the floor and waited, hoping the sounds would come to me."

Regent didn't want to encourage her, but he asked anyway. "Did they?"

"No. You came in, and it was over."

He wanted to ask what kind of drugs she had in her backpack, but that seemed harsh.

"Well, what do you make of it?" he asked.

"Huh?" She didn't understand the question at first. "Oh, I see what you mean. It's simple. They were ghosts."

"Ghosts?"

"Sure. Based on what you've told me about this house, I'd say it's bound to have ghosts. The only questions are what kind and who and why they are here tonight and what they're doing."

"Ghosts?" Regent asked again. The way he spoke made it more statement than question.

"You sound skeptical, Professor. I'm really very surprised at that. I would have thought..." She didn't finish.

They sat quietly for a moment, each trying on a new understanding of the other.

"As you know, Professor, I'm a writer. I haven't published much, but I do write. And as Gabriel Garcia Marquez said, a writer is someone who can believe anything."

She waited for him to respond, but he didn't.

"Those were ghosts," she said with finality. "Haven't you encountered them before?"

Regent thought about Liam. He still wasn't sure what to make of Liam.

He mentally crossed his fingers and said, "Not to my knowledge."

"I bet they've been here, even if you haven't seen them."

Regent had had all he could handle for one night. He put his plate and glass in the sink, and together they made their way back upstairs.

They walked quietly, not speaking, so they wouldn't wake Scap and Nurse. On the second-floor landing, Jane put her hand on Regent's arm and stopped him.

"Listen," she whispered.

They both heard it – voices. Low and soft. They came from the back of the third floor.

He motioned to Jane to follow him, and they tip-toed toward the sound. As they came closer to a small sitting room at the back, the voices became louder. And then there was another sound – cards being shuffled.

Regent smiled, trying not to gloat. "Sounds like your ghosts are playing cards."

He pushed open the door to reveal Scap and Nurse, she in an old corduroy bathrobe of his and a pair of his wool socks, Scap in a red flannel night shirt, thin from many washings, and a sweater. Nurse was dealing. Scap turned his cards over one by one and frowned each time.

"Hey, Delia. We've got company."

So now it's Delia, not Nurse, Regent observed.

"I hope we didn't wake you," Nurse said. "I couldn't sleep, so I made some Ovaltine and came back here to watch the moon and clouds. Scap woke up, too. We've been playing gin rummy and reliving old times."

They were so jolly, they filled the room with good feeling.

"Who's winning?" Jane asked.

"Let me put it this way," Nurse said. "I don't think Scap can afford to play much longer. He now owes me $1.15."

"Deal the cards," Scap said.

Nurse giggled like a young girl.

Chapter Five
Slumber Party

"It's funny how none of us could sleep," Scap said.

"Isn't it, though," Jane said, turning her head a little to one side and arching one eyebrow.

"I woke up because I was hungry," Regent said.

"Really?" Jane said. "And when was the last time you got so hungry that it woke you in the middle of the night?" She glanced down the length of his long thin body.

He pulled back one side of his mouth and rolled his eyes a little.

Jane turned to Scap. "What woke you?"

"I'm not sure. It was like someone came to my bed and shook me. Like it was time for me to get up and do something."

"It was the same with me," Nurse said.

Regent's discomfort rose a notch.

He said, "Jane, here, was wakened by ghosts."

His sarcasm either went unnoticed or it was ignored purposely.

"Probably was," Nurse said. "We used to hear them all the time when Franklin Manor was a cure cottage."

"Did anyone ever take pictures of them?" Regent asked.

"No, of course not," Nurse answered evenly. "You know it's not possible to take pictures of a ghost."

"Oh, that's right, I forgot." More sarcasm. He knew he shouldn't talk that way to Nurse.

"Well, it's clear then. We were waked up by ghosts," Jane said. "The question is why. And why are we gathered here in this cozy room in the middle of the night?"

"It's not hard to understand," Nurse said. "But first you have to realize that they aren't ghosts. They're angels. In the cure cottage days, we thought of them as ghosts, but after the nuns moved in, the so-called ghosts served them with such constancy that their presence and their true nature became apparent. They were – still are – angels."

"OK, so they're angels," Jane said. "That still doesn't explain why they called this meeting."

"I don't know why you and the professor are here, but as for Scap and me – well, they wanted us to get reacquainted. It's been years since we've spent any time together, and it has been so very pleasant to sit up late chatting. It was a gift to us."

"Yeah," Scap said, smiling broadly. "Like being teenagers, only better. And, of course, you, Delia Broussard, had the added pleasure of winning all my money."

"I'll let you pay it out in installments," she said, suppressing a grin.

"I have a better idea," Scap said. "When I get my next social security check, I'll take you to The Antlers, and we'll do some old-time dancing."

Nurse had been looking down as she put the cards back in their box, but when he said that, she looked up quickly toward the wizened little man in his red night shirt. She may have flushed a little, but Regent had turned off most of the lights, so it was difficult to be sure of that.

The moment passed, and the four of them, angels in attendance, moved along into the kind of easy conversation that is usually reserved for old friends. They talked about stories in the *Eagle* and village life during the war and the winter carnival that was coming in February and other matters that were at once inconsequential and bonding.

Jane shuffled the cards and played solitaire and said little. She looked happy to listen.

At a break, she did say, "Could I interest everyone in a game of hearts? Nobody seems ready for bed yet."

"Now you're whistling my tune," Scap said eagerly. "I'm good at hearts."

Regent surprised himself with his response. "I'll go get drinks."

Nurse and Scap had Ovaltine, Jane herbal tea, and Regent decaf. They played for a long time. Scap was, as he'd said, good at hearts.

Eventually, the rush of energy they'd been feeling began to subside, and they put away the cards.

"Uh, Professor, I've been thinking," Nurse said.

"Yes?"

"Well, you know, this house is quite large, but you invited Scap and me to stay, and if Jane stays too, well, I've been recalling what it was like here when there were twenty-five patients and a staff."

Regent waited, trepidation growing.

"In that situation, things were pretty regimented. Meals at regular times. Bathing on a schedule. Maids and nurses assigned to particular jobs. That sort of thing."

Regent looked at Jane, expecting her to bristle with disapproval. She didn't.

"There were a lot of rules, but they made it possible for us to live together in harmony. I was thinking that maybe we could use a few rules now, so we don't wear out our welcome with you, Professor. You've been living alone a long time. So has Scap. I don't know about you, Jane."

Jane smiled and said nothing.

Regent's first reaction was characteristic. No doubt Nurse meant well, but he had the sense that his own life in his own house was about to be structured by a committee.

Nurse continued as if she had read his mind. "It's your house, Professor. You've been so gracious in taking us all in. Why don't you tell us what you'd like in the way of, you know, how we get through our daily affairs. That would be ever so much better than guessing."

Her words made sense, but they also made him uncomfortable. To give her what she was asking for would require a level of openness far beyond his custom.

"Oh, I don't know."

"She's got a point, Professor," Scap said.

Even Jane Felsher Kravitz, onetime student rebel, nodded in agreement.

"You're all very thoughtful," he said, "but we're doing OK like we are, aren't we?"

"Come on, Professor. Give this a chance," Jane said. "Of course, I myself am not going to be here long, but while I am here," she grinned, "I know to stay out of your record collection. But don't make it hard for these two to be your guests."

Scap said, "It sounds like good sense to me, Professor."

They waited in vain for him to respond.

"Did you have anything specific in mind, Nurse? "Jane asked.

"Well, I was thinking we could start by agreeing on a daily schedule of who is responsible for shopping, cooking, and cleaning."

Jane turned to Regent. "What do you think, Professor?"

"It's OK, I guess," he said. Then he added, "provided," – he paused then said it again – "provided I have complete control over the schedule, and I alone make the rules." It took them a moment to realize he was joking.

The way their chairs were placed, Regent was the only one who had a view to the east.

Abruptly he said, "Would you look what we have done." He drew it out, emphasizing each word, and pointed.

Off the room where they sat, was a cure porch with many windows. It looked out into a stand of winter-bare maples and a bit farther on white pines at the edge of the village cemetery. The others turned to look. The first light of a new day was filtering through the trees.

For a while, they sat in silence, watching the changing colors of the rising sun reflect off the snow. Then, as the outlines of the gravestones became visible, a bell began to ring. It filled the house. After a few moments, it stopped. When its echo had died away, they stood as one and processed silently to bed and peaceful sleep.

Chapter Six
"Oh, Wow"

If having meals at appointed hours was to be part of the new regimen, it hadn't begun yet. On this day, breakfast got under way when Regent came down at around 11:00. The others showed up at intervals over the next hour.

Regent was drinking coffee and reading a book, when Jane came in. She took a seat across from him and stirred honey into herbal tea.

Probably going to talk, he thought. If they were going to have rules, they should start with *Regent's Rule* No. 1: at breakfast – whatever time it is – no one talks until Professor Regent gives the OK, and on some days, he might never give it.

Scap came in next.

Through a yawn, Jane said, "What was that, Professor?"

"What was what?" He kept his eyes on his book.

"The bell, of course."

"I don't know. Just a bell."

"It was Liam's bell," Scap said. "You remember it from Christmas Day, don't you, Jane?"

"Not clearly. I was bleary from the pain medicine. Who is Liam?"

Regent thought about whether something needed his attention in another part of the house.

Scap answered. "Liam was an altar boy at the public Masses in the monastery. Last week, he gave the Professor a replica of the full-size one that hung in the monastery."

"And?"

"And it rang at dawn."

"Spontaneously?"

"Not likely. It was probably rung by an angel to remind us it was St. John's Day."

"What's that?"

"Well, see, the day after Christmas is St. Stephen's Day, like in the carol about King Wenceslaus, and the next day, the 27th, which is today, Catholics remember St. John the Apostle, who was Jesus' favorite, and the patron saint of love, honor, and friendship."

"Why do you need reminding?"

"In Oliver's Mountain we have a special way of observing the period between Christmas and Epiphany? Do you know what Epiphany is?"

"Well, duh. Even we half Methodist, half Jews know that."

Scap explained it to her anyway. "It's when the wise men in the east followed a star to the infant Jesus in the manger."

She was tempted to tell him that epiphany was also a literary term associated with James Joyce that means a moment of seeing things in a new way. She let it go.

Scap continued, "and around here we join the journey of the wise men, which gets going in a big way on St. John's Day."

"Oh, wow," Jane said.

What's she going to say next? Far out?"

"I've got to see that bell, Professor," Jane said.

"I'm not sure where it is."

"You're not sure where it is? A bell with that much juju and you don't know where it is?"

"It's here somewhere," he said. Then he added, "Jane, I have a different – more rational – view of the bell than Scap and Nurse."

"OK, then what do you think happened last night?"

"I don't know, but I'm sure there's a rational explanation."

"The bell's in a red and green box in the parlor," Nurse said.

When Jane returned a few minutes later, she said, "I didn't find the bell, but Dick came to the door, before I finished looking."

It was another relatively warm day, but Dick was still wearing his arctic expedition gear.

"How y'all doing today?"

"Want some coffee, Dick?" Regent asked. *Maybe if Dick got started, they'd quit talking about the bell.*

"How are you, Dick? Making any headway with your story?"

Chandler didn't answer. "Is there any more of that turkey? Could I make a sandwich? I'm hungry."

He made a big sandwich and ate it quickly. When he finished, he took his plate to the sink, and came back with a handful of cookies and another cup of coffee.

"Boy, all this food is making me sleepy. Could I go upstairs and take a nap?"

Without taking a bath?

"Sure, why not?" he said. He knew why not. Set this guy's imagination loose in this crazy house with its unexplained noises and such, and no telling what he'd come up with.

Jane showed Chandler to a small room that had the name St. Gemma Galgani on the door. Except for a single bed Regent had bought at a yard sale, it was unchanged from when the nuns were in residence.

"You're lucky," Jane said, examining the varnished woodwork, roller shades, and vivid blue, post-Vatican II paint. "My room is decorated in unfinished sheetrock."

"Uh huh," Chandler said. He stripped to his long underwear, fell on the bed without turning the covers down, and shut his eyes.

"Well, good night, Dick." She spread a blanket over him, lowered the shades, and left the room smiling.

When she got back to the kitchen, the other three were going over a housekeeping schedule Nurse had drafted.

Nurse was going to make dinner the rest of the week. She would do lunch, too, except that it would only be cold cuts and salad served buffet style on the sideboard. At that meal, each person would wash his own dishes. Scap would set the table and clean up after dinner. At breakfast everyone was on their own. Laundry, cleaning, and other jobs were yet to be assigned.

Regent had other kinds of order in mind, but he kept them to himself. First, of course, there was *Regent's Rule* No. 1 – no talking at breakfast until he gave the go-ahead. In addition, they would gather for cocktails or tea at 5:30 each day. But there wasn't much whisky left, and he didn't have money to buy more. In fact, he was wondering how he was going to afford groceries. Since he'd gone broke, he'd been living mostly on his social security checks, and that didn't permit playing gracious host to long-term guests.

Scap said. "I've observed that the Professor likes to have a drink before dinner. I do, too. And if memory serves, Nurse enjoys a sherry now and then. I don't know about you, Jane."

"I don't drink."

"Well, you can have tea or a soda –"

Regent interrupted him. "That's a good idea but..." It took him a moment before he could continue. "But I can't afford it. I'm sorry. Sorrier than you know." His face flushed a little at that last bit of intimacy.

Nurse said, "Scap and I were talking about money last night, when we were playing gin rummy. We have a proposal. He and I will provide a petty cash fund for groceries and household expenses and important things like sherry and whisky."

Regent tried to protest, but she cut him off. "You provide this wonderful house, Professor. That's quite enough."

"Uh oh," Jane said. "I have no money at all. I mean not any. Zilch"

"Don't worry about that," Regent said.

"I'll be right back," Nurse said. She went upstairs, moving slowly but with grace and assurance. Regent went into the kitchen and stood at the sink, staring at the wall. Jane and Scap sat in silence.

Nurse returned with two shoeboxes. "I found these in a closet. We can keep the cash in one. When someone goes to the grocery store or pays for something else in cash, put the receipt in the other. I don't think there's a need for any careful bookkeeping. It should be enough just to keep receipts so we'll have them if we need them."

Regent agreed to do it their way, but he had misgivings. He didn't like taking their money. As a man of a certain age, he should be able to offer them bed and board free of charge. Besides that, Nurse and Scap probably didn't have much to share. And even if the three of them pooled everything they had, it probably wouldn't get them through the next maintenance emergency.

"Who wants to do the shopping this week?" Nurse asked. She held up her chart and pointed to a blank on it.

"I'll do it," Jane said.

Nurse checked to see if everyone liked what she was planning to cook, then handed Jane a list.

Regent watched Jane reach into the cash box. To his and Jane's astonishment, there was a sizable pile of bills there. Quite enough to cover groceries and whisky, too.

Jane took several bills and left.

Chapter Seven
Scap Does His Annual

"Professor, I was wondering... " Nurse said.

"Yes?"

"Uh, do you remember, you said you would help me with Ferdie?"

"Of course I remember. It's not every day that I offer to wrest a damsel from the clutches of an evil relative by becoming her guardian." *Especially not one I've only just met.*

"Well, I talked with Preston Butcher this morning. If you're still willing, he's got some papers for us to sign."

Regent was still willing, but he'd been thinking of spending the afternoon in solitude, reading. "Now?"

"Preston says it's important that we get started right away."

Scap shoveled enough of the driveway so they could get out and warmed up the car while Regent dressed. At the office, he didn't read the documents or pay much attention to Butcher's description of their contents. It was enough to know that by becoming Nurse's guardian, he would destroy her great nephew-in-law's power over her. Ferdie would no longer be able to confine her in the back room of his house. And he wouldn't be able to control her finances.

Regent signed the papers quickly, and left Nurse in the warm office while he went to get the car.

He drove to the front door and waited. After ten minutes or so, he was about to go in and see if anything was wrong, when she emerged. Butcher walked her to the car.

"Goodbye, Preston. I'll keep you posted," she said. "Sorry to make you wait, Professor. We had another matter to discuss."

"It's OK." He realized that he had begun to worry about her. At her age anything could happen.

On the way home, he stopped at the Post Office to pick up his mail. It consisted of some catalogs and a registered letter. He knew what it said without opening it. That did not reduce its power. Just looking at it made his stomach churn.

Since he'd gone broke, the mortgage payment had been a haunting presence. He could put it out of his mind from time to time, but it was always there, perched like a gargoyle on the eave of a big church. But not one to fend off evil. Rather, evil itself.

He'd gotten behind in payments before, but by very careful budgeting, he'd always managed to catch up. Never so far behind as now, though. The note had a graduated interest rate, and it had increased to the point where he was simply unable to keep up. Half a per cent didn't seem like much, but on a note the size of his, it increased the payment more than he could absorb. So now, here it was. Foreclosure action would begin at the end of January.

He walked slowly back to the car and drove home saying nothing.

It was as if he'd been suddenly wakened by a very loud noise. What had he been thinking? How had he dared to enjoy the holidays and friends? He'd been very foolish indeed.

And now he had three houseguests who were planning to stay – at his invitation – for an indefinite period. Driving along between streetside snowbanks, he imagined the constable evicting him and scattering his new friends to God knows what kind of situation. Whatever had possessed him to become this old lady's guardian? And it had been *his* idea.

At the house, they found Chandler sitting in the parlor yawning over a book. Regent wanted very much to be alone. And if he had to talk with someone, this strange man, Dick Chandler, would not be the one he chose.

"Hello, Professor," Chandler said.

"Dick." Without slowing, Regent moved along the protective runner from the front door to the mudroom to take off his boots and hang up his coat. Chandler followed him.

"I'm finding Oliver's Mountain to be rather strange," he said.

Oliver's Mountain is finding the same about you.

Chandler didn't require a response. "While you were gone, the doorbell woke me up. I went down and saw Scap talking with some children. Looked to be about junior high age. He put on his coat and boots, and they all went off down the street."

This time Regent managed a response, though it was quite small. "Uh huh."

"Scap said he was going to do his annual. What does that mean?"

"Afraid I don't know. Ask Scap." Regent had finished in the mudroom and was halfway up the first flight of stairs.

"I think I may know already," Chandler said. "I wanted to see if you did and would talk to me about it."

Will this man ever let me alone? Will he force me to be rude?

"I don't know anything about it."

Nurse had finished taking off her things and was standing in the mudroom doorway listening.

Chandler went on. "I heard the children say, 'Oh hello, Mr. Goehring. We heard you had moved over here. Who will it be this year?'"

"What did Scap say to that?" Nurse asked.

He said, "Let's go see Ferdie Roscoe."

"What?" Regent exclaimed. "You must be mistaken. He wouldn't go near Roscoe."

"I'm telling you what I heard, Professor."

"Impossible," Regent said.

"Not at all, Professor," Nurse said. "It would be just like Scap to do that." She smiled as she spoke. Regent examined the smile for irony or bitterness. There was neither.

"I don't get it, Nurse. Why would he go there? And why do you look so happy about it? I would think you'd be angry."

"I'm very proud of Scap," she said.

"I don't understand," Regent said with some heat.

"I don't either," Chandler said.

. "I'm sure you don't," she said.

"Will you explain, then?" Regent asked.

She thought a moment, then shaking her head said, "When the time is right, you'll understand. Now I'm going to have a rest. I'm really quite tired from last night."

Regent went up the stairs behind her, leaving Chandler standing at the bottom, looking puzzled.

Chapter Eight
It Is What It Is.

Even before he picked up a yellow pad and started jotting ideas, it was clear. He'd have to find a way to do two things. Both simple. Both difficult.

First, he'd have to stall the lender. Some version of "the check's in the mail." He couldn't think right off what might work, but there had to be something.

Then he'd have to find a way to make some money. He knew how he could do that, but he didn't want to. He'd almost rather flip burgers at MacDonald's. Still, it was what he knew best, and in the circumstances, there seemed no other choice.

As things stood now, he would lose more than the house. That alone would be painful, but he'd get through it. What was one more failure? But now, he had Nurse and Scap and Jane to think of as well. A half smile crossed his face. And if he lost the house, where would Chandler bathe and nap?

First thing in the morning, he would contact the community college and the several prisons in the area about a teaching position, and he'd look into substitute teaching at the high school, all the while hoping he would somehow be spared from more teaching.

With that, Regent set his notepad and pen on a bed table, took off his glasses, lay down, and closed his eyes.

It was almost dark when he woke. He washed his face and was about to go downstairs before he thought better of it.

If the temperature weren't dropping so rapidly and so much, he would take a walk and not stop until he came to terms with things. But it would soon be too cold for that, so he settled for cocooning in his old chair and gazing down on the village and mountains spread out before him in the day's last light.

As always, the scene was restorative, and he was beginning to get his nerve back, when someone knocked softly at his door.

It was Nurse. "We were about to have our little cocktail hour, but we didn't want to start without you."

"Huh? Oh. OK, I'll be right there."

He brushed his thin hair, changed into a tattersall check shirt, and pulled from a drawer an old cardigan with threadbare elbows. It was his at-home version of business casual. As usual, it made him feel more in control.

His new friends had found a tray, and on it were Old Fashioned glasses of fine crystal, mementos of a more prosperous time. There were pretzels and nuts in little bowls. A fire was crackling on the hearth.

He raised his glass and said, "Cheers." It felt good to be with these people. It was going to be awful to lose this.

Chandler took Regent's thoughts in a different direction.

"Scap, what does 'doing annuals' mean?"

"Oh that's right, being from somewhere else, you wouldn't know. It's a local custom. Something we do during the Twelve Days of Christmas. We go around and either try to make things right with people we've gotten crossways with during the past year, or we just go out and do some little acts of kindness that we've been too busy or too unthinking to do at other times."

"Oh, wow," Jane said.

"Does everyone do this?" Chandler asked.

"Oh no," Scap said.

"Who then?"

"I don't know. I've never thought about it. Some people do, and some people don't."

Chandler turned to Regent. "How about you, Professor? Do you participate in this custom?"

"Not me. This is the first I've heard of it."

"Now that you do know," Chandler said. "Will you participate?'

"It doesn't work like that, Mr. Chandler," Nurse said. Still not using his given name, Regent observed. "People do annuals when they're ready, and being ready involves more than just knowing about it."

"It's like joining a club or being confirmed in the church or something – is that what you mean?"

"I mean it is what it is. You'll be wasting your time to try to figure out what causes people to do this."

Chandler looked unconvinced. "Well," he drawled. It sounded like he had said "wail." "Let me see if I can at least understand what you did this afternoon, Scap. You and those kids went to this Ferdie person's house to make amends for something?"

"No, not quite that."

"What then?" Jane asked, her eyes wide with interest.

"Nurse's nephew, Ferdie, has treated her terribly for the past several years. He's been keeping her as sort of a prisoner. Taking all her money. And so on. When the children showed up today – I've done annuals with them ever since they were old enough – Ferdie seemed like a good place to start."

"Sounds more like a good place to vandalize," Jane said. "But you didn't do that, did you?"

Scap smiled and shook his head. "Of course not."

"So, what did you do?" Jane said impatiently.

Regent, too, felt impatient.

"Well," he paused. "We knocked on his door, and when he answered, we asked him how he was doing and if all was well with him and then we wished him a merry Christmas and a happy new year and we left."

"Why?" Jane, Chandler, and Regent said in a loud chorus.

"A less deserving person would be hard to find," Regent added.

Scap sighed. "It just seemed like the right thing to do. It's what happens in Oliver's Mountain at this time of year."

"I don't understand," Regent said. Jane and Chandler looked like they didn't either.

Chapter Nine
Poems in the Parlor

"Join us for dinner, Dick?" Regent said it unenthusiastically, though not exactly reluctantly.

The whisky, followed by turkey soup with dumplings and a green salad, took Regent's mind off his money problems. But toward the end of the meal, worries reappeared. He excused himself before the others were finished and went to St. Gertrude of Nivelles, the partially renovated room he used as a study.

He took a seat at his desk and stared at the wall. It was an article of faith with him: look at the wall long enough, and words would come. In this case, he would think of something to say to the bank that would put off foreclosure until he could find a way to catch up the payments. After a good deal of staring and thinking, he started to type. He littered his desk and much of the floor with discarded drafts, before he finally had what he wanted – a direct appeal.

He asked for more time, suggested a payment schedule, and then, rather creatively in his view, included his resume and a list of places where he was going to apply for work. He emerged from the room resigned but somewhat less fearful than when he had entered.

He spent the next couple of days enjoying not being alone in the house, and his hopes of getting the bank to work with him grew. But the likelihood that they would not was never far from his mind.

One evening he came down from his room and encountered a scene in the parlor that took him where money was not an issue. Scap and Nurse were sitting very close to each other on the couch. Jane was on the floor in half-lotus position. And Chandler stood as if on stage, his back to the fire, reciting poems. Regent stayed out in the hall so he wouldn't interrupt.

Chandler's audience looked enchanted, like children around a campfire. And no wonder. He was performing the Robert Service ballad, *The Killing of Dangerous Dan McGrew*. Whatever its shortcomings as art, it did have rhythm and imagery and some hard-to-identify ingredient that most people respond to.

But I want to state, and my words are straight,

and I'll bet my poke they're true,

That one of you is a hound of hell ... and that one is Dan McGrew."

Then I ducked my head, and the lights went out, and two guns blazed in the dark; And a woman screamed, and the lights went up, and two men lay stiff and stark;

Pitched on his head, and pumped full of lead, was Dangerous Dan McGrew.

"Oh, hello, Professor," Chandler said. "I let it be known that I have a fair amount of poetry committed to memory, so they asked me to perform some. *Dangerous Dan* was Scap's request. It's your turn now. Is there a poem you'd like to hear?"

Regent thought a moment. He'd not make it too difficult. No obscure Ezra Pound *Canto* or anything like that. No point making it too easy, either. Everybody could recite a Shakespeare sonnet or two. *Prufrock* was what he felt like hearing, but that seemed off key following *Dan McGrew*. In the end, he said, "Oh I don't know, Dick. Just give us one of your favorites."

"Sure. Any restrictions? Anything off limits?"

"Not on my account," Regent answered.

"All right then. I'll give you a religious poem I like – a short celebratory prayer by the nineteenth-century Jesuit priest, Gerard Manley Hopkins.

Glory be to God for dappled things – for skies of couple-color as a brinded cow; for rose-moles all in stipple upon trout that swim...

When he finished, no one said anything for a while. The silence was finally broken by Scap. "I've never heard that one before, but I like it. What's that line again about "stippling?"

Chandler said it again.

"That sure is what trout look like, all right. I wonder if that Father Hopkins ever fished the Au Sable. It's a great trout stream."

Chandler smiled. "Hopkins lived in England a long time ago, so he didn't do that. But – "

Jane interrupted. "You can't be sure though. Think about it. He was here in this room with us just now."

"You have a point," Chandler agreed. "Hey, Hopkins makes me think of Psalms. Y'all want to hear some? I know all of them. I found an old prayer book one time, and I didn't have much else to do, so I learned them."

"All 150?" Regent asked.

"Yeah."

"Really?" Regent didn't doubt him, but it was the only response he could think of.

As if to back up his claim, Chandler began. "I'll give you one I like a lot – Number 27. *The Lord is my light and salvation. Whom then shall*

I fear...." When he finished, he recited a few more, including some less familiar ones.

"How is it you know so many poems, Dick?" Regent asked.

"I just like to memorize things. I seem to have a knack for it."

"Nobody would argue with you on that," Jane said.

"I can recite the Louis Untermeyer anthology, too."

"All of it?" Jane asked.

"Most of it." He said it as if he'd told them he was able to tie his shoes. "Shall I do some for you?"

Without waiting for an answer, he began with Frost's *Mending Wall.*

Regent pulled the Untermeyer collection from a shelf and suggested titles for the next half hour or so. During T.S. Eliot's *Journey of the Magi*

A cold coming we had of it,

Just the worst time of the year

For a journey, and such a long journey...

Regent had a sudden realization. How had he missed it? How had Jane missed it? This man had asked to take a bath and a nap, and he'd been very hungry. Was he sleeping in his car? Did he even have a car? How far had he come to get here? Being directed in a dream to come here was not unlike following a star. He'd ask Dick about it sometime.

After the Eliot, Regent said, "I'm going to bed now. Dick, if you want to stay over, use St. Gemma Galgani, where you took a nap."

"That's real generous of you, Professor. I am enjoying being here. If you're sure..."

Regent wasn't sure. But he said, "Make yourself comfortable." It was a step short of "make yourself at home," but it would have to do.

"Thank you very much. And I wonder, Professor, if I could use your computer?"

Regent couldn't think of an acceptable way to refuse. It wouldn't do to say, "I don't let anyone use my computer." Certainly not after the man had so endeared himself with his recitation.

"It's in my study, St. Gertrude of Nivelles, in the back on the second floor."

"Do all the rooms have saints names?"

"Most of them. They were here when I moved in, and I haven't bothered to remove them. Haven't really wanted to, as far as that goes."

"Do you know who they are?"

"Just the same ones everybody knows – Mary Magdalene, John the Baptist, and I can't tell you a lot about even those two. I've never bothered to look up any of the lesser known ones like Gemma and Gertrude."

Late as it was, Regent had one more thing to do before turning in. He went to the mudroom and put on coat, gloves, and a wool cap.

As he reached the front door, Jane and Nurse, who were still in the parlor, looked at him curiously.

"I'm expecting a visitor," he said. He let them chew on that for a moment, then added, "Lately, a cat – a big one judging by his footprints – has been coming up on the porch during the night to have a look around. His tracks start at the street, come up the driveway, then up onto the porch. He stops to look in the parlor window, then goes on all the way to the other end."

"Cats are mysterious creatures, aren't they," Nurse said. "I love that about them. Haven't had one in years, though. Why don't you catch it, Professor? If it's a stray, well..." She paused. "Sorry, it's your house. I didn't mean to presume."

"Don't be silly. That was my thought, too. But there's a problem."

"What's that."

"I've never seen this cat, and – "

'He comes when you're asleep," Jane interrupted, laughing.

He gave her a look, and said, "Oh Jane, you always were a quick study. And you haven't lost a step. So, one of these nights, I'm going to stay up and see if I can make friends with him. But he doesn't come every night, so I might sit up several nights and still not see him. I'm interested but not that interested."

"What are you doing now? You going out to look for him before you go to bed?"

"No, I'm just going to brush the snow smooth on the porch, so that he'll leave clear tracks if he comes tonight."

Chapter Ten
Pawprints

On his way down to breakfast, Regent stepped out into the frigid air of the long front porch. Jane was already there. She held her arms folded tightly over her breasts and shivered.

"Good morning, Professor." Without unwinding her arms, she pointed with one finger at the snow near her feet. "He was here. Maybe tonight we could take turns staying up to watch for him."

"We could, but I've thought of an easier way. I'll get a Have-a-Heart trap. Don't know why I haven't thought of it before." He had thought of it before, but he hadn't wanted to spend the money.

"You can put it down there where the tracks end," Jane said.

He looked where she was pointing with her head. "Uh huh."

"Is that all you have to say, Professor?"

"It is."

"What about the abrupt way the tracks end? They just stop."

From the parlor window the pawprints made a straight line toward the south end of the porch. Then they ended. It looked exactly as it would have if the cat had levitated.

"You must have asked yourself why," Jane persisted.

Regent raised his eyebrows, opened his mouth a little, paused, then said, "It's cold out here. Let's go have breakfast."

In the dining room, Nurse, Scap, and Chandler were sitting at the table having coffee, leaning forward, and talking, softly and intently.

"Good morning, everybody," Regent said.

The three at the table straightened up and responded more or less in chorus. They seemed half startled.

Chandler folded some pieces of paper that were on the table in front of him and put them in his shirt pocket.

"Did the cat show up, Professor?" Nurse asked.

"He did. I'm thinking I'll try to trap him in one of those cage-type traps, if I can find one that doesn't cost too much."

"I know a guy who'll loan us one," Scap said.

"Oh, great. Thanks, Scap. Hey, did everyone sleep well? I don't know about you, but I'm still feeling the effects of that all-night card game."

A general "fine, thanks" sort of response followed.

For the next several minutes, conversation was desultory and, Regent sensed, a bit awkward.

Over a second or third cup of coffee and blueberry muffins, it got a little easier.

Nurse said, "Professor, before you came in, uh, we were talking. I was telling Scap and Dick" she'd started using Chandler's first name, Regent observed "about the plan you mentioned last week of turning this house into an artists' colony like Yaddo."

Regent felt his face grow hot. How could this subject come up now, just when he was facing foreclosure?

"It seemed like a very good idea, to me – a fitting new incarnation for this house that has long been a historic force for good. Are you still thinking about it?"

He took a moment to gather himself. "Yes and no. It would be wonderful, but it would take a lot of money, and I don't have any."

No one responded for a while.

"On the other hand, I guess I have a pretty good start on a kind of Yaddo already. Here we all are at the breakfast table. We've just enjoyed a fine evening of poetry. I plan to spend much of this day reading. Tonight we may add a cat to our merry band. So, money or no, a community of kindred spirits seems to be coming together naturally."

"But do I understand," Nurse asked, "that, if you had sufficient money, you'd still like to operate the house as some sort of artists' colony in a formal way?" Nurse asked.

"Sure."

"How would it work?" Chandler asked.

"I don't know. Even when I had money, I never got very far with plans. I mostly just imagined scenes – evenings pretty much like last night. Maybe a lecture now and then. Sometimes musical performances. Accomplished people living here. Talking ideas and art sitting by one of the fireplaces in winter, gathering on that long porch in summer."

"How would you select residents? How long would they stay?" Chandler asked eagerly.

"I haven't decided yet, but if I won the lottery, I'd buy champagne and some cheeses and bake some bread – it happens that I make a great baguette – stoke the fire in the parlor, and we'd sit down together, and you'd help me make some plans."

His eyes grew bright with the thought, and he smiled broadly. The others smiled, too.

But all the while Regent was describing the vision, he was sure it would never happen. When he stopped speaking, hopelessness came over his face like a cloud had scudded in front of the sun. It did not go unnoticed. No one spoke for a bit.

Scap broke the silence. "Why don't you ring the bell?"

Regent's answer was to turn down the corners of his mouth and tuck his chin into his wattle in an expression that was an effort to reject Scap's suggestion without being overtly disagreeable.

"You've seen what that bell could do," Scap said.

Before Regent could answer, Chandler asked, "What did it do?"

"Got us a fine Christmas dinner, a load of firewood, and a bottle of good whisky," Scap said matter-of-factly.

"What?" Chandler said, looking puzzled.

Jane said, "Damn. I have got to see that thing. I'll go look for it again."

She ran up the stairs, her feet barely touching the treads. She came down at the same sprightly pace.

"Looks like you're getting over your accident," Regent said. "You're moving very well."

"Yeah, I feel much better." She handed him the box.

He set it on the table without opening it and concentrated on his coffee.

"Aren't you going to ring it?" Jane asked.

"Oh, c'mon," he said. He left off, "*Leave me alone. Why are you doing this to me?*"

"What's the risk?" Jane continued.

"No risk. It's just not who I am."

"Not who you are?"

"That's right."

They all looked at him for a time, saying nothing.

"OK, OK. So, you'll let me alone, I'll do it."

He lifted the top off the box and pulled out several layers of tissue paper.

"One problem, though." He paused for effect. "It's not here." He held the empty box out for them to see.

Scap hurried up to the parlor almost as quickly as Jane had.

Regent had mixed feelings. If the bell was lost, maybe they'd stop pestering him about it. On the other hand, the bell had become a part of his life and the house, and he wasn't quite ready to be without it.

"Have you had it out since Christmas Day?" Nurse asked.

"I haven't."

Scap returned, saying, "It's not anywhere in the parlor."

For the next hour or so, all of them, including Chandler, went room by room looking for it. They didn't find it.

In the end, Scap said, "It's here somewhere. We just haven't found it. It's here. The nuns sent it to you by a special messenger, and they would not take it away."

"I do wish we had found it," Regent said. "I was so looking forward to drinking that champagne and having our planning session."

"You shouldn't make fun, Professor," Jane said sharply.

"I'm sorry. It's just that I don't feel the same way about the bell as the rest of you do. I apologize."

There were murmured acceptances, and for a while no one said anything. Then Nurse said, "Professor, I need to see Preston Butcher again. Could you drive me there later?"

"And if you'll drop me at my buddy's house, I'll get that Have-a-Heart," Scap said.

"Better get a good one," Jane said. "That's a really clever cat."

Chapter Eleven
Plans

Nurse and Scap persuaded Regent that a small observance of New Year's Eve was in order. So he made baguettes, while they set out olives and nuts, crumbly North Country cheddar (for Scap) and Camembert (for Regent). The aroma of the baking bread drifted up the stairs filling the ground floor like incense in an old church

"Is that bread, I smell?" Preston Butcher exclaimed as he let himself in. "How about champagne to go with it?" He held up two bottles. "Happy New Year."

"Oh, hello, Preston. What a nice surprise. Happy New Year to you," Regent said.

"I forgot to tell you I had invited him," Nurse said. "When I was at his office yesterday, we got to talking about one thing and another, and it came to light that there's a grant program, which supports projects such as your Yaddo idea. It sounded very promising to me, and since the deadline for applications is coming up soon, I asked Preston to come by, toast the new year with us, and help us get going on it."

"You don't say. And did you bring a check back with you so we can finish renovating the house before it collapses?" He surprised himself with the sharpness of his tone.

"No, of course not," Nurse replied patiently. "I did bring hope and eagerness, though. You might try some of that." An old lady's rendition of a sassy smile played at the corners of her mouth.

"Well, let's get started, then," Regent said a little sourly.

Butcher popped the cork on one of the bottles, and as the wine bubbled out, Regent caught up with the spirit of the moment.

He raised his glass. "Here's to our success," he said in a voice that was stronger and more assured than any of them had yet heard from him.

They all raised their glasses.

"First, let me give you a little background," Butcher said. "The foundation is probably different from any you've ever encountered in that the benefactor wishes to be anonymous. As the administrator of funds, I'm the public contact, though I have no role in making awards."

"What's the name of the foundation," Chandler asked.

"North Country Charitable Trust."

Chandler, Jane, and Regent all spoke at once, each with a different question.

Butcher didn't respond to any of them. "All I can tell you is that its purpose is stated broadly – 'to support the arts and improve life in the North Country.'"

He poured more champagne and helped himself to bread and a slice of cheddar.

"Very good bread, Professor."

"Thank you, Preston. It's been a while since I've baked much, but I'm thinking I'll start doing more."

"Let's have a look at the application form," Jane said to Butcher.

"There isn't one. The benefactor asked me for advice on this point, and I recommended two things. Keep it simple and allow the applicant to be creative. I've always thought the best way to interview someone for a job – applying for a grant is pretty much the same as applying for a job – is with a single inquiry. 'Tell me why I should hire you.' So, to be considered for a grant from North Country Charitable Trust, all you have to do is make a case in writing for why it should fund you."

"That would be easier if we knew who the benefactor was," Regent said.

"You'll have to manage without knowing," Butcher said.

"Does this person or persons live around here?" Jane asked.

"No comment."

She tried again. "Political affiliation?"

"I've told you already. The benefactor wishes to remain anonymous." He refilled glasses. "Uh, if you don't mind me saying so, you really should get started. Time is of the essence."

Jane didn't need any encouragement. She was excited. "What's the purpose of your Yaddo, Professor? I've made a few grant applications. They always require a mission statement. Even peculiar grants like this one."

He shrugged. "I think I told you earlier. I just want to provide a place to live for people who are engaged in the arts in some way." He thought for a moment about Nurse and Scap. "Also, people who are curious. Good conversationalists. Well-mannered. That's about it. Some or all of the above."

"But to what end?" Jane argued. "Hey, Dick, take notes."

I am" He tapped a finger to his temple.

This assertive and energetic Jane was the person Regent remembered from her student days – not the one he'd found a few days earlier living on the street.

Jane persisted. "What's the point of getting such people together here, Professor?"

"The point? I've never really thought about it in that way. If I had to, I suppose I could think of some reasons, but I've reached a point in my life where I feel free to do whatever I want, so long as it does no harm."

Jane showed her disapproval by much shaking of her head.

"Let me ask another question then," she said. "Maybe this one will get you focussed. What are you going to call this thing?"

"Well now I have thought about that. For about fifty years this house was given to curing the sick as Franklin Manor Sanatorium. For fifty years following that, its role was to provide spiritual sustenance as the Carmelite Monastery. If we get this grant, it will assume a third incarnation for good as, for want of a better term, an artist's colony called Franklin Manor III."

The discussion became lively and animated. How many residents? How were they to be chosen. Would they come for defined periods or could they stay indefinitely? What would be required of residents?

Jane, Scap, even Chandler had definite views on various issues. Regent remained resolutely determined not to be specific.

Nurse said little, except on one matter. They had come to a sticking point regarding the mechanics of recruiting and selecting applicants.

Regent said, "When I thought I would fund this with my own money, I imagined that people would just find their way here more or less naturally." He looked at each of them in turn and made a slow, sweeping gesture with his arm. "That's begun to happen already. I imagined that I would say yes or no to people coming here without having to define my criteria of judgment. Same for level of financial support. I would give more to those who needed more and less to those who didn't need as much."

Jane became increasingly assertive. "But Professor," she said loudly, "a foundation is not going to give you money just to play around with any way you feel like."

Nurse disagreed. "I don't agree with you, Jane. The little we know about this trust shows it to be quite unusual. I would not be at all surprised if it permits the flexibility the Professor requires."

"Not a chance," Jane said. "That is not how grants work. Believe me, I've had experience with these things."

"I'm sure you have," Nurse responded. "But if spelling out the details of the operation in the way you're suggesting is something that is too different from the Professor's dream, then I say don't do it."

Regent said, "Dick, when you write up the notes, include this – 'Selection of residents and amount of financial support will be solely at the discretion of Dr. Regent.'" After a stand-up comedian's three-beat pause, and half smiling, he added, "'in consultation with friends already in residence at Franklin Manor.'"

If he meant to lower the tension, he didn't reach Jane. What had been just a strongly held opinion turned suddenly into hot anger. "You're making a big mistake," she almost shouted. "You're throwing away a wonderful opportunity." She searched for words for a moment, then gave up, and stalked out of the room and up the stairs.

"Perhaps you should leave off for now," Butcher said. "It's getting late."

Butcher saw Nurse up to her room. After a few minutes, he came down and said goodnight to Scap and Regent, who were on the porch checking the placement of the cat trap.

"That should do it," Regent said. "Tomorrow, Tom will start the new year with a new life."

Chapter Twelve
Disappearances

Regent was in bed pursuing the great white whale and smoothing out after the evening's excitement before crawling into his mummy bag on the porch.

"You awake?" Chandler said as he knocked.

If I wasn't before, I am now. Franklin Manor III is not such a good idea if it means I can't be undisturbed in my own bedroom.

"Come in, Dick," he said, trying not to sound resigned.

He stayed in bed, his book on his chest.

"I typed up my notes, and I thought you might like to see them."

Surely this can wait till morning. His thoughts must have showed.

"Oh, they'll wait, but there's something else I was hoping we could talk about."

Regent cringed inwardly. It sounded like a prelude to intimacy.

"I have some questions about the village, and I wanted to go over them with you before I go down and work on my story."

"OK. But if I fall asleep in mid-sentence, don't take it personally."

"Oh, sorry. Maybe tomorrow."

"No. That's all right. Let's talk. What's on your mind?"

He stifled a yawn.

"Well can you tell me more about that magic bell? I gather that y'all rang it on Christmas Day and here came a big ol' dinner, firewood, and whisky right out of nowhere. Is that true?"

"It's true that the one followed the other. Whether the first *caused* the second is quite another question." *One I'm not going to answer.* Chandler must have sensed that, because he didn't press it.

"Well, tell me this. Where'd you get the bell?"

"From a man named Liam."

Chandler raised his eyebrows in a way that said he expected Regent to go on. He didn't, so Chandler prompted him.

"Who was he?"

"Liam was an altar boy here when the house was a monastery."

No matter what the next question, that was as far as he was going. There would be no discussion of the detail that when Liam had showed up, he'd been dead for years.

Neither man said anything for a time. The conversation was pushing Regent to think about things he preferred to deny or at least keep at a distance. He hoped Jane had not told Chandler about the cat's disappearing pawprints.

"And what about the ringing y'all heard at sunrise the other day?"

"I can't explain it, Dick. Like Nurse said, it just is what it is." Regent's aversion to talking about these mysteries was overlaid with a sense of proprietorship. These things Chandler was asking about were a private matter.

"I sure do wish I could have seen that bell."

"It's probably around somewhere. This is a big house. Really more of a building."

"Professor, we looked a long time. We were systematic. It's not here."

"I can't imagine where it went then," Regent said.

Then he cleared his throat in a way that those who knew him well recognized as an announcement that a professorial moment was coming.

"Listen, Dick, I think you may be reaching. Trying to find more mystery than really exists. In my view, any village – any house for that matter – is going to have a little of the extraordinary and inexplicable mixed in with the otherwise unremarkable events of daily life. If I may say so without sounding pompous, that's how life is, and there's nothing to be gained by dwelling on it."

Before Chandler could respond, they heard a noise from the front porch.

"Aha," Regent said. "That's the door on the cat cage. Let's go meet Tom."

The tracks went from the driveway end of the porch, took a little side trip over to the parlor window, then went the whole length of the porch and to the front of the trap. Its door was closed. The bowl of food they'd left inside the cage was empty.

"This guy is obviously feral. Could be a little out of control, Dick. So let me open the cage." He held up his heavy mittens for Chandler to see.

The overhead light on that end of the porch had burned out, and the cage was in shadows. They bent close to the opening, and Regent said, "Don't be afraid, Tom. We just want to say hello. You're only moments away from a nice bowl of cream."

He reached in slowly trying not to alarm. The cage was about three feet long. He felt around near the opening, then carefully slipped his hand toward the back. Must be smaller than his tracks indicated, Regent thought. When he reached the end of the cage, he became less tentative and swept his arm from side to side. The realization came to both of them at once. The trap was empty.

"Clever fellow," Regent said jauntily.

Chandler was looking at the snow in front of the trap. "Clever is right. There are no tracks leading away. His tracks just end."

"Yeah. Sure do, don't they." Regent said.

"Oliver's Mountain is getting more interesting all the time," Dick said.

"I've got to turn in now, Dick. Good night."

* * *

They had finished a special New Year's brunch and were ready to clean up the kitchen, but Jane had still not come down.

"Reckon we should leave any of this food out for Jane?" Chandler asked. Boy, the guy has moved right in, Regent thought.

"I'll go see if she's OK." Nurse said.

She was gone for some time.

"I'll check on them," Regent said.

He found Nurse coming down from the third floor.

"She's gone."

"Gone?"

"That's right. I checked her room. Her few things and her backpack are missing. She's nowhere in the house."

"Well, that's not good," Regent said. Instantly, realization of how fond he was of Jane came over him. It had been a happy fortuity to catch up with her again. "She got so angry last night. I hope she didn't leave on account of that."

They talked around the event in fits and starts as they cleaned up the breakfast dishes. When they were finished, Scap said, "Since Jane's gone, I'll do the shopping." I think the store will open up around two."

Nurse made a list, and he got out the petty-cash box.

"Uh oh," Scap said.

"What is it?" Regent asked.

"Yesterday afternoon, this box had the week's remaining grocery money in it plus some extra. When Jane handed me the change to put away, there must have been a hundred dollars or so there. Now..."

He turned the box upside down and shook it. It was as empty as the bell box.

Chapter Thirteen
Sister Julia Responds

They refilled their coffee cups and tried to come to terms with what had happened. There was a good deal of sighing, but words were slow to come.

When Regent had known Jane some years earlier, she'd been hard working, ambitious, and curious. She was the unusual student who made the teaching-learning connection work in two directions. Some teaching amounted to the instructor conveying information and the student receiving it, but the best teaching had energy going back and forth between them in a swirl of nudging and growing and changing. That's how it had been with Jane.

By being polite the past few days and waiting until she was ready to talk, he might have done her – and all of them – a disservice. It might have been better to probe and prod a bit about how she'd come to be living on the street. If she was at the point of stealing friends' grocery money – and that seemed to be the case – she had needed to talk.

Scap said, "I've been robbed a couple of times. It always makes you feel real bad, even if the thing that got stolen wasn't very valuable."

Nurse raised her eyes from the spot on the table she'd been staring at and looked intently at Scap, but said nothing. The others stayed silent too.

"You never know what's inside someone." Scap went on.

"So you think Jane took the money?" Chandler asked.

"Sure. It's obvious, isn't it?"

Whatever his private thoughts, Regent wasn't having it. "Hold on, Scap. You didn't see her take the money, did you?" He didn't wait for an answer. "She didn't leave you a written confession, did she? All we know is that Jane left during the night. And the grocery money is gone."

"I'm sorry, Professor. I know she was a friend of yours."

"No, Scap. She *is* a friend of mine."

"Sorry," the old man said again. "But you'll have to admit, it doesn't look good."

"Indeed, it doesn't," Nurse said.

Regent's head popped back as if he'd been punched. *Surely not Nurse, too.*

But then she added, "And that's all the more reason for us to withhold judgment. That's what one does."

"For how long?" Scap asked.

"As long as you are given grace to believe. Forever, if possible."

"Knock, knock," Sister Julia said as she entered the dining room. "No one answered the door, so I let myself in."

"Oh hello, Sister," Regent said. "You know where the coffee pot is." He gestured toward the kitchen with his head.

She poured a cup and joined them at the table. Regent introduced her to Chandler, then said, "It's good to see you, Sister." The warmth of his feelings surprised him.

When the nuns had left Oliver's Mountain, Sister Julia had stayed behind to take care of her ill brother. She had been responsible for the monastery's maintenance, and on several occasions, she had showed up unexpectedly to help Regent when something had broken.

"To what do we owe *this* visit?" Regent asked, grinning. "I think everything is working all right."

"I heard the bell."

Regent waited for someone else to respond. No one did. This was beginning to be a little much for him. He was tired of the bell and the levitating cat and all the rest of it.

"That's interesting," he managed finally. "Maybe it will ring again while you're here, and that will enable us to find it."

"What do you mean?"

"It's gone."

"You've just mislaid it," she said with finality. "I heard it."

"You heard it, but we didn't?" Regent said.

Sister Julia smiled but said nothing. Her expression said she had no difficulty believing that had happened and that if Regent couldn't believe it, well, he simply didn't understand the true nature of things.

"I saw Jane early this morning when I was out walking my brother's dog. What's going on with her?"

"You tell us," Regent said. "What was she doing?"

"Getting on the Trailways bus."

"Did you talk to her?"

"Didn't have a chance. The bus pulled out as soon as she got on. What's the story?"

They told her what had happened.

"I can ask Sam Arnold down at the station where she was going," Sister Julia said.

Regent answered quickly. "I don't think it matters. What about the rest of you?"

They agreed with him.

"Then let's just leave that where it is, and as Nurse says, do the best we can not to think badly of her."

Sister Julia changed the subject. "Say, that sure is a good looking cat out there on your front porch. And big. About the size of a bobcat."

"You saw him?" Regent and Chandler said in chorus.

"Well, yes. When I came up on the porch, it was standing on its hind legs looking in the parlor window. When it saw me, it came over and rubbed on my legs."

"Oh. I thought you might have seen the cat we've been trying to catch. But if the one you saw was friendly, it was a different cat," Regent said.

Nonetheless, they hurried upstairs to have a look. They crowded through the door eagerly and stopped. Out on the front steps sat a very large tabby, his tail curled around his paws.

"Well, hello Tom," Regent said. "You *must* be the guy we've been trying to catch. It's not possible there could be two cats so big."

Quite calmly, Tom looked at each of them in turn, then stood up and did his best to shake the snow off his coat. He had little success, since it had suddenly begun to come down heavily. Seeming to ignore them while actually being fully on guard against them, he sauntered up onto the porch, slowly walked to the far end, turned around and came back the other way, moving magisterially, like a priest processing in at the start of Mass, and descended the steps onto the driveway.

Regent turned around to face the others and raised his hand in a stop-sign gesture. "Everybody wait here." Then he moved off in quiet pursuit. As he stepped off the porch, the snow began to come down more heavily.

The cat went up the driveway along the side of the house toward the backyard, continuing to move in the same ceremonial way, his tail up and waving like a tour guide's flag. "Stay with me," it said. Big floating flakes were now coming down so thickly that Regent had to increase his pace to keep him in sight.

When the cat reached the back of the house, he took a few steps out into the yard and sat down in the deep snow, still and calm as a house cat on a warm hearth. When Regent drew near, Tom raised his head. The two looked directly into each other's eyes for a long moment. Regent reached down to pet him, but at the last instant before contact, Tom vanished – without noise and without movement. He simply was no longer there.

Regent jerked his hand back as if he'd touched something hot, then looked around quickly to see if his friends had followed. He needn't have worried. The snow had reached near whiteout force, so even if they were close behind him, they probably would not have seen what happened.

He stood motionless in the swirling whiteness and gathered his thoughts. Probably – surely – he had simply lost sight of the creature.

Pawprints were still faintly discernible. They led to where Tom had been sitting. Regent kneeled and searched for prints that led away. There were none.

Keeping his hand against the side of the house for guidance, he felt his way back to the front porch.

"It looks like he got away," Scap said.

"Yeah. Went over the fence and across the street. The last I saw of him, he was heading into the cemetery."

Chapter Fourteen
A New Plan

The snow had started so suddenly and was coming down so heavily it made everybody vaguely uneasy.

"I'll make some more coffee," Nurse said. They followed her down to the kitchen, where they stood and watched the pot.

"That's a lot of snow," Chandler said.

No one disagreed.

"How about I stoke up the parlor fire?" Scap said. "Keep old man winter at bay."

"Sure," Regent said unenthusiastically. He might go to his room and leave them to enjoy it without him.

As Chandler stood with his back to the smoky restart of the fire and looked out the window, he said again, "Yep, sure is a lot of snow." The porch was all he could see. Beyond it was impenetrable whiteness.

"I hope that cat has a warm place to sleep," Nurse said.

"I wouldn't worry about him," Regent answered.

"Well, why on earth not?" She spoke in what, for her, was quite a loud voice.

"He just seems like a cat who can take care of himself, that's all."

"Uh huh." She didn't seem at all persuaded.

"How do you know it's a he?" Sister Julia asked. "Did you get that good a look?"

"It's just a way of speaking, Sister. We geezers are quite comfortable with the arbitrary assignment of gender. It's not a statement of fact regarding the cat's anatomy."

If his sourness bothered Sister, she didn't show it.

"I think it's time that cat had a name," Scap said. "He's always hanging around. Might as well call him something and let him, you know, really be a part of our little group."

"I already gave him a name," Regent said. Giving names was a prerogative he would not share. It was an essential element of owning a grand historic house.

"He does? What is it?" Scap asked.

"Tom."

"My that's original," Scap said, grinning.

"It's perfect," Regent answered. "He gets an ordinary name because he's an ordinary cat." Before Chandler could contradict him, he added, "Hey, enjoy your coffee. I'm going up to my room."

He shut the bedroom door, settled himself in front of the window, stared at the flat light of the whiteout, and thought about Tom, the "ordinary" cat.

He'd probably imagined the sudden vanishing. Must have needed a little drama in his life. It had to be that he had simply lost sight of him in the squall. Yeah, that was it. And the tracks suddenly ended. They'd probably just gotten covered by the new snow. But that didn't explain the times when the tracks on the porch had disappeared in the same abrupt way.

Another thing. It seemed like Tom had sat down and waited for him. As if he wanted to say something. Actually, he had said something – in a way – with that undeniable eye contact.

Regent shook his head like a dazed boxer.

Well, what if the cat *was* an unfathomable mystery? Why should that matter? Life was full of mysteries. Professor Regent couldn't find an answer for that. Didn't even try very hard. He didn't like such things, and that was that. He just wouldn't think about it.

But he couldn't keep from feeling low. His financial situation was grave. Gazing into the curtain of white, he sank into hopelessness.

It had been very pleasant to dream away an evening drinking champagne and discussing possibilities with his new friends. Getting financial support and establishing a Yaddo had seemed like something that actually might happen. For two or three hours, it was as if it already had happened. It didn't seem that way now. He felt foolish.

Even if the trust did make an award to him, the money would be slow in coming. That's how grants worked. The mortgage lender would take the house back before he received the first check. In the light of day, especially this impenetrable white light, it seemed extremely unlikely that the bank would give him time to catch up. They wouldn't be persuaded by his plan to go back to teaching. Even if they were that gullible, he himself wasn't. He'd been out of teaching for some time, and that would work against him. There might not be openings. If there were, they would probably go to younger people.

No, it was time to get realistic about his prospects. Franklin Manor III was a dream he'd never realize. Oh well, he'd had a life before he'd bought the house. He would have a life after.

Maybe he'd move to Florida, rent an efficiency apartment, live on his social security and meagre savings, and take long walks on the beach. There would never be another dog as good as Maalox, but maybe – if he could find the courage – he would get another one. Give up entirely on human friends. They were one more thing he couldn't afford. And anyway, he didn't seem to have the knack for friendships.

When Jane was a student, she had been a friend. Then she'd left for her mother's funeral and hadn't come back. This second installment with her had been even more disappointing. She'd disappeared just like Tom. At least Tom hadn't robbed him. Nurse could urge them all she wanted not to reach hasty judgments, but in the privacy of his own thoughts, he knew what had happened. Some other time, some brighter time, he'd ask himself what had driven Jane to do such a thing. Looking out at the snow, he only felt abused.

He turned his chair so that he was squarely in front of the window. He would sit there staring into the blinding illumination of the whiteout, until he came to a better place.

After a time, an impulse came to him that brought an acerbic smile to his face.

If he could find it, he'd ring the bell. Provided, of course, he could do it without anyone knowing.

But the bell was not going to be found. Maybe Jane had taken it along with the grocery money. Even if she hadn't, the thing was not in the house.

As he had many times in recent months, he thought about selling the house. It came to nothing, though. There was little demand for such a structure; it would take too long to find a buyer. Even if he did, in its half-renovated state, the house would not sell for enough to pay off the mortgage.

It came to him finally what he had to do. Unwelcome as it was, there was some relief in knowing.

He would send a second letter to the lender, telling them it was his intention to default. Just get it over with. He'd call his guests together and tell them they'd have to leave. He'd complete the guardianship procedures, so that he could keep Nurse free of Ferdie's bullying. She seemed to have some money. He didn't know how much, but surely she could afford an apartment of some sort. Maybe she and Scap could pool their resources and share one. Chandler, well, Chandler was on his own.

He moved the chair back to its corner, lay down on the bed, and in the way people do when exhausted by grief, fell immediately into a deep sleep.

When he woke two hours later, the snow had stopped.

He got a cup of coffee from the kitchen, took it back to his room, and began thinking about how he would put it to his new friends that they would have to find somewhere else to live. He rehearsed several formulations, but never found the right words. After a time, he went to St. Gertrude and drafted the letter to the bank. He printed a copy, which he would look at again before mailing.

At lunch nobody had much to say. They had soup and grilled cheese sandwiches and talked about how it was good the snow had stopped, and then they were done.

"Hey, Professor, I've been thinking," Chandler said as they were taking dishes to the sink. "Do you have a camera?"

"Well, yeah." *Doesn't everyone?*

"I was thinking, why don't we put some food in that trap and try to take a picture of Tom when he comes back. We could use a trip wire attached to the shutter release. What do you think?"

"We know what he looks like. Saw him this morning. Why do we need a picture?"

"It's not what Tom looks like that we're after. It's how he manages to go in and out of the trap without getting caught."

"Uh huh."

"And if we're lucky, maybe we can get a picture of his disappearing act."

Regent shrugged. "OK. I'll get it for you."

Chapter Fifteen
The Photographs

Regent spent the next day as much alone as he could without seeming rude. Anyway, brooding about the letter and having to tell his new friends made him too self-absorbed to be good company.

The morning after, he woke early like he always did, but not eagerly. He stayed in his mummy bag a while, then dressed slowly. A cup of coffee in hand, he went out to look at the trap. As before, tracks led to the door, and it was shut. Regent opened it and looked in. The food was gone, but the cage was empty.

"Ah, Professor, I was about to wake you. Look at these." Chandler held out some prints.

Regent took them to the vestibule and held them up under the overhead light. He turned them one way and then another. Neither of them said anything.

The trap and pawprints were perfectly clear. But there was no cat. There was something else, though. Regent looked at Chandler.

Chandler shrugged his of shoulders. Regent turned the photographs around a few more times.

Around what would have been Tom's neck was some kind of necklace. Suspended from it was a bell.

"Well," Regent said.

"Is that the same bell y'all been talking about?" Chandler asked.

"Nah. Couldn't be," Regent said.

"I bet it is," Chandler said.

Regent didn't respond.

Chandler followed Regent to his study, where they drank coffee and watched the sun illuminate the gravestones in the cemetery. Little by little, it filtered through the trees behind the house.

"This is a real nice place to work, Professor."

"Yes, it is."

The sheetrock walls still awaited sanding and painting, but that was small distraction. As home offices go, it was uncommonly large. Ornate trim and dentil molding below the cornice gave it an air of grandness. Large double-hung windows took up most of two walls, bringing outdoors into the room.

"What do you make of it, Professor?"

Regent shrugged. He made a lot of things of it, but he didn't want to say any of them to Chandler. Or to anyone else, for that matter. He could not deny that mysteries were as much a part of the house as leaky plumbing, but that didn't mean he had to talk about them. Certainly not to a writer. Do that and pretty soon tour buses full of gawkers would start arriving.

"Who are you writing your story for, Dick?"

"Whoever I can get to take it. I'm not on assignment."

"Oh, that's right. I believe you said, you were directed to come here in a dream."

"I was."

"You do magazine work? Books?"

"Whatever I can."

"Would I have seen any of your work?"

"Not likely."

"Why is that?"

"It's hard to explain."

Regent waited a moment to see if he was going to try. He didn't.

"So, what do you make of the photographs?" Chandler asked again.

"I don't know. That probably isn't a bell at all. Bad lighting. Something like that."

"You don't believe that, Professor."

"I don't?"

"No."

"What I believe might surprise you."

It was now full daylight. A classic Adirondack-blue sky caused Regent's spirits to rise, despite his burdens.

He stood up and bent forward over his desk so he could see the porch thermometer.

"I'll never get used to the way these beautiful clear days in winter are often much colder than the gray ones that seem more threatening. That," he raised his eyes upward, "looks like a summer sky, but it's minus 14 out there. This is the kind of day when people are misled by appearances and get frostbite on their ears when they walk to the grocery store without covering up."

Chandler looked at him without responding. He waited for the professor to go on. He gave the impression that he would wait as long as necessary for the evasions to stop. If that was meant to draw Regent out, it didn't work.

"I think I hear the others, Dick, and I need a little solitude, if you don't mind. This is the time of day when I make journal entries and get myself together."

"Sure," Chandler said again.

As Chandler was leaving, Regent said, "Leave the camera with me, and I'll try to make better prints."

"Sure."

Regent deleted the photos on the camera and put the prints Chandler had made in his pocket.

These are sock-drawer material, Regent said to himself.

With that, he put Tom out of his mind.

He spent the rest of the morning checking one last time the letter to the bank and preparing what he would say to his new friends. He looked at the wall for a long time, trying to persuade himself that he needn't feel so bad about them and that really, he was not obligated to provide shelter for them. He didn't succeed. But the house had worn him out, and it was time to admit defeat. He'd tell them at lunch.

He was about to drag himself down to the dining room, when Scap knocked.

"Professor? You in there? You got a FedEx delivery."

"Thanks, Scap. I'll be down in a minute."

The flat cardboard mailer held a letter from the bank.

Probably want me out by sundown.

"Dear Dr. Regent. Regarding your loan, No..."

He was pretty sure what the content was going to be, so he skimmed it rapidly. In the last few lines, he found something he didn't expect. "You may disregard our previous demand letter."

It didn't make sense. This response had come too quickly, and it was too agreeable. Lenders didn't act that way. But his questions soon gave way to relief so strong it made him short of breath. The terribly hard words to Scap and Nurse that he been rehearsing would never have to be spoken. At least not yet.

He spent a full ten minutes looking at the backyard and its winter-bare maples and the white pines that lined the cemetery across the way, coming to terms with where he was now in regard to the house, his obligations, and his plans.

At lunch, Scap said, "It must have been good news in the FedEx package. You look pretty happy."

"Oh, just a routine business matter," Regent said.

"Say, Dick was telling us about those pictures of Tom. This old house has a lot of mysteries, doesn't it."

"I'm sure there's a rational explanation. We just haven't figured out what it is yet."

"Oh, c'mon, Professor. You know better than that," Scap said.

The look on Nurse's face and the way she was shaking her head indicated that she agreed with Scap.

Scap went on. "Whatever you think, Professor. But I say, it's great to know that the bell is still here, even if it's hanging around the neck of a mysterious cat."

"Uh huh," Regent said.

Chapter Sixteen
Reading Lesson

As they were finishing lunch, Regent said, "I don't remember who's on the schedule for cleanup, but let me do it. You guys go take a nap or something."

Nurse looked at him with a puzzled expression and began carrying plates to the sink.

"Hey, c'mon Nurse. I'll do these. You've been doing more than your share. Come to think of it, why don't I make dinner tonight?"

She protested, but he would have it his way. He'd take a long celebratory walk and stop by the store on the way back. Make his favorite dinner – meat loaf, mashed potatoes, and green beans. His one-rise bread. Ice cream and frozen blackberries for dessert.

Sidewalks had been cleared of the big buildup from the previous day, so he could have walked, but on consideration, snowshoeing and taking a circuitous route seemed the better choice. Lately, he hadn't had enough energy for it, but on this day he had more than enough.

It was only two blocks to the start of a trail that wound around a medium-high mountain offering several choices among difficult inclines and easier trails. By choosing the latter, he could stay out a couple of hours and still not get too tired.

He moved along rhythmically, enjoying the blue sky and bracing air and being alone.

It was remarkable how quickly things could change. Suddenly he had time to make up the arrears in his payment. He'd be able to get a teaching job, and he'd learn how to like it. Now all he needed was for the grant to come through, and he could get on with life in a most agreeable way.

Too bad poor Jane couldn't have stayed with them. He should have talked with her. Maybe there was something he could have said or done. She must have been very troubled.

The exercise brightened his outlook, and he entertained the possibility that she might somehow be – what was the word – "rehabilitated?" That didn't sound quite right, though. Whatever the word, perhaps there was some reasonable explanation for what she'd done, and somehow, she would one day return. Probably not, but, on the other hand, good fortune had been a big part of his life recently. Maybe it would continue.

After he got back from the store, he put the groceries away, and humming – not something he did much of – went to check news headlines and weather on his computer.

He found Chandler was at his desk pecking away on the computer keyboard. That settled it. As soon as he could find time, he would install a hasp and padlock on the door.

The letter from the mortgage company lay open on the desktop next to the draft of his intention to default.

"Oh, hello, Professor." He stood up quickly and moved away from the desk.

Regent nodded and put the letters in a drawer.

Regent was unwilling to lose the happy feelings he'd been having, so he made an effort not to be annoyed.

"Listen, I don't mean to pry. I just came to use your computer, and I couldn't help seeing your letter to the bank. I'm sorry about what you've been going through."

"It was nothing I couldn't manage."

"I don't doubt that. But isn't it great you have the support of friends at a time like this?"

Regent was confused. He was not aware that his friends had known about the mortgage problem.

"And your benefactor must love you very much."

Regent let it go. "Uh huh."

"Do you know who did it?"

"Did what?"

"Caught up your mortgage payments."

"What are you talking about, Dick?"

Chandler looked puzzled. "The FedEx letter…"

Regent read through it again – this time carefully. It might have been a different letter from the one he had skimmed a few hours earlier. The first time through, he'd found what he wanted, even though it wasn't there. The lender had not agreed to the catch-up plan he had initially tried to get them to accept. Instead, someone had made the overdue payments for him, and his mortgage was now current.

Regent read it through two more times. It made no sense. It was like he'd won the lottery without having entered it. He had no wealthy friends. In truth, he didn't have many friends of any kind. And few relatives. He could not imagine who would have made the back payments for him.

He picked up the phone and punched in the numbers on the letterhead.

"Louise Matthews speaking."

He gave her the reference number on the letter and said, "I'd like to know, please, who made the payments on my account."

"I'm sorry, Dr. Regent, I can't tell you that."

"You can't? Why not?"

"Such information is confidential in any circumstance, and in this case, these payments were specifically conditioned on the donor remaining anonymous."

Regent continued pressing Ms. Matthews, but she would not tell him anything. He hung up in annoyance.

Chandler said, "Want me to see if I can find out who your benefactor is?"

"I don't know how you'd that, but, sure, give a try."

"The bank will be closing in a few minutes, but I'll go over tomorrow." As he prepared the meatloaf, Regent thought about little else. He put it in the oven along with the bread and went up to join Scap and Nurse for drinks. Sister Julia was there, too.

"I understand you've had a piece of good fortune, Professor," Sister Julia said.

"What's that?" He wasn't going to assume she was privy to his affairs. She'd have to own up to it.

"The mortgage payments."

"Oh. Well, yes, I have."

"Who did that for you?" Sister Julia asked.

"Beats me."

"You don't have any idea at all?"

"None at all. Dick is doing some sleuthing, but I don't expect him to succeed."

"Whoever it was, it's wonderful that it happened," Sister Julia said.

Nurse had gone over to brush some ashes back into the fireplace. As she returned to her chair, she put her hand on Regent's shoulder and gave it a little squeeze. "I'm very happy for you, Professor. I haven't liked thinking of you in such distress."

"You mean you knew?"

"Well, yes, we all did," Nurse said.

"How?"

"Dick told us."

"Oh?" *Dick has been pretty busy lately.*

Regent was furious, and it extended to all of them, not only to Dick. He didn't like the violation of his privacy, and he didn't like being an object of their concern. In his ideal world, he was the giver of concern and kind understanding, not the recipient.

"Don't be angry. He said that when he used your study that evening after we'd discussed the grant application, several drafts of your letter to the lender were lying around. He couldn't avoid seeing them."

Regent struggled to keep his temper, and it showed.

Sister Julia said, "Professor, I see you didn't learn as much at Christmas as I had hoped."

"I beg your pardon," he said, frowning and trying hard to remain civil. It wouldn't do to yell angrily at a nun.

"You had some problems, and your friends were concerned about you. Then someone anonymously took care of your mortgage. You hate being in that position, don't you. I thought you might have learned that even a self-sufficient former professor cannot live in isolation. It's OK to need others. In fact, that's the human condition."

He rolled his eyes and allowed himself an angry retort. "Sister, I'm quite aware of the human condition, thank you."

"Sorry, I don't mean to be patronizing. But in your pride, you are missing something important."

He waited.

"We would have been glad to help you."

"Really? And how would you have done that?" he said, his voice loud and his eyes wide. "I only needed one thing: a large amount of cash. Perhaps, I'm wrong but – "

Sister Julia interrupted. "That's far from all you needed. You needed the warm encouragement of friends as much as you needed the money. Maybe more."

He smelled the bread and meatloaf, and it gave him an opportunity to break off the talk before it escalated into rude argument.

"I need to see to dinner," he said and started for the kitchen.

"Professor, I won't allow you to be angry with us. We're your family, don't you know?" Sister Julia said.

He stopped and looked at each of them in turn. He was not willing to go entirely by Sister's rules, but in the face of their earnest good will, his anger lessened.

"Thank you, Sister. Will you join us for dinner?"

The next day, they were having lunch when Chandler arrived. "Anything left?" he asked. "Snooping makes a guy hungry."

He made a sandwich, then with his mouth full he told them about his investigation.

"I started at the logical place."

"The bank," Scap filled in.

"That's right. I asked to see that Miss Matthews you talked to on the phone, Professor."

"I'm sure she opened up and told you everything, didn't she," Regent said.

"In a way she did. As I hoped, she still had your file out on her desk. When I saw it, I suddenly felt ill. Fainted dead away. She rushed out to get me a drink of water. When she got back, I felt better, and the first few papers in the file had moved mysteriously into my coat pocket. After I faint that way, I always need to go to the bathroom. While I was there, I read the papers."

"Well, let's have them." Regent held out his hand.

"I'm not a thief, Professor, I'm an investigator. After I finished in the bathroom, I dropped the papers on the floor under Miss Matthews' desk when she wasn't looking."

They sat quietly and waited.

"Well?" Regent said finally.

"Your benefactor was a Ronald Jasper."

"Ronald Jasper," Regent repeated.

"None of you know who that is?" Chandler asked. He looked at them one by one and waited.

No one knew him.

"On the way back, I googled him on the library's computer. He's Jane's uncle."

Chapter Seventeen
Regent Makes a Decision

Regent groaned like he had been struck with sudden pain. "You're sure of this, Dick?"

"Positive."

"And you left all the papers in Ms. Matthews' office?"

"Yeah."

"I don't suppose you could go over there and get sick again, this time be a thief, or at least a borrower, as well as an investigator? I'd like to read the bank's records in detail."

"I don't know if I can do quite that, but I'll try to get you some more information. Hey, what's the matter, Professor? You act like this is bad news."

Regent shrugged and said nothing.

Sister Julia shook her head knowingly. "This is where I came in. You were reaching the point where you could accept an anonymous gift, right Professor? But you have trouble taking one that's probably from Jane, who is your friend. That's how it is, isn't it."

"I simply don't want to be beholden. Nothing wrong with that."

For a while, no one said anything.

Finally, Nurse said, "This gift will result in a lot of good. Because of it, your Yaddo is now once again a possibility. Not to mention," she smiled impishly, "none of us will have to look for another place to live."

Regent saw her point, but it was far less important than his desire not to be rescued by Jane.

"I'll say goodnight, now," he said.

In the morning, he turned to more snowshoeing to get his thoughts straight. He stayed out a long time. When he returned, he was worn out, but he had a plan.

Ms. Matthews was polite though a bit impatient when Regent entered her office.

"Thank you for seeing me," he said. "I'll come right to the point. I want to return the money that was paid on my behalf."

"Oh?" She looked puzzled. "In my many years with the bank, I've encountered nothing that was at all like the anonymous gift or your request, but off the top of my head, I'd have to say I'm pretty sure it's not possible for you to return the money."

"Why not?"

"Because your account has already been credited, an agreement signed, and so forth. I can't imagine how this arrangement could be undone."

"I can't accept that, Ms. Matthews. No disrespect, but may I talk to your superior?"

She phoned someone and explained the situation. The answer was still no. Regent appealed to still higher authority.

Ms. Matthews walked him down the hall to a corner office.

"This is quite irregular, Dr. Regent," bank president Shaftesbury said.

"I'm quite aware of that," Regent said dryly.

Shaftesbury read the file.

"Sorry, we can't do it."

"You're absolutely certain?"

"Yes, I am."

Regent reached into his worn leather briefcase and pulled out the letter that he had drafted earlier but not mailed.

"This is to notify you that I will make no more payments on my loan. You may start foreclosure action whenever you are ready."

"That's a bit hasty, isn't it, Dr. Regent?"

"Not at all. In a sense, I've spent my whole life working up to this."

"I don't understand," Shaftesbury said.

"It's about integrity," and, he admitted to himself, about being stubborn.

That evening after dinner, when they were all in the parlor, he told his friends where things stood.

"I have some difficult news. The mortgage lender is going to foreclose on the house after all. You'll have to find another place to live. I'm sorry, but there is no other way."

Chandler was the first to speak. "I don't get it, Professor. I thought Jane's uncle had gotten you caught up?"

"I can't accept that. I tried to get the bank to return it to him, but it won't. So, I have informed the bank that I will make no more payments on the loan, and they can foreclose whenever they like."

"But since you're current now, won't it be several months before they actually do foreclose? Why shoot, anything could happen during that time. You might get that grant, for example," Chandler argued.

"The one thing that would have to happen is that the money Jane arranged for her uncle to give me would be returned to him. I cannot live here as a beneficiary of her charity. It was quite a large amount of money. God only knows how she persuaded uncle to give it to me. And I can't even find her to pretend I'm grateful."

Despite the Professor's clinched-jaw resolve, his friends would not give up. They all stared at the fire for a time, each gathering himself and trying to find persuasive words.

Scap was the next to speak.

"Professor, I think it's time to ring the bell."

"Despite what you might think, I *would* ring it, if we could put our hands on it. Nothing would come of it, of course, but I know you all would like that, and it would do no harm. But" he said it again, this time with more emphasis, "BUT we no longer have it. It has left as mysteriously as it came to me."

Scap wouldn't let it go. "It'll turn up, Professor. You wait and see. And when it does, things will change."

"No. No. It's time to give up on this house and give up on the bell. Sooner or later, one must live life realistically. Tomorrow, you'll have to start looking for an apartment. The bell is gone."

His friends sat in silence for a time, then one by one they left the room.

Chapter Eighteen
The Story of the Bell

Regent sat for a while looking at the fire, brooding and wondering how his life had come to this. Soon the day's emotional ups and downs joined forces with fatigue from the snowshoeing, and he nodded off. The fire burned down to coals, and the room grew cool, causing him to stir a little. He came full awake when a strong draft of cold air swept in as the front door opened.

He looked up and sucked in his breath in alarm, but with a part of himself he was not at all surprised.

"Hello, Liam."

"Hello, Professor. You need to put some wood on that fire. It's cold in here."

"I'm sure you know where the woodpile is. You've known everything else."

Liam soon returned with an armload of logs. Regent watched morosely while he rekindled a blaze.

"What brings you here, this time, Liam?" Before Liam could answer, Regent had a thought that cut through his anguish and made his heart beat faster. "Did you bring me another bell? And – "

Liam cut him off. "Not exactly."

"Oh."

"Planning to give up the dream, are you, Professor?" It was as much statement as question, a way to elicit confirmation that Regent was participating in the conversation.

"Uh huh. It's time. Did you come here to talk about that?"

"Not exactly."

"What then?

"I wanted to tell you a story."

"Long or short?"

"Medium."

"I presume it's a good story, one that justifies my being up at this hour to hear it."

"The best story I know."

Liam smiled broadly and crooked his big head to one side.

"What does that look mean?" Regent asked.

"Nothing. Let me start."

A long time ago, when the nuns first took up residence in this house, they had to get along without just about everything. For several months they didn't even have a bell to use at Mass. When the bread and wine were elevated, they made do with a little set of three hand-held bells that just jingled. Nothing wrong with that, but it didn't announce to the village in a loud voice the presence of God, the way a deep-throated bell in a tower would.

Well, at their first Christmas Eve Mass in this house, a miracle happened. It was a very cold night as usual, but bright and clear. Every star in the sky shone with special brightness, as if to bless the celebration.

I was serving that night. As we approached the point in the Mass when the priest was to hold up the bread, I reached down for the little set of jinglers, but they weren't there. I looked all around where I was kneeling, but I couldn't find them. What was I to do? I couldn't say to the priest, "wait a minute, Father, while I look for the bells." I didn't know what to do.

Father kept going. He raised the bread – and then it happened. The lights in the house dimmed, and a bell boomed from the cupola over the icehouse. The sound seemed to set the whole house vibrating. It filled the village. It resonated off Oliver's Mountain and came back across the lake with an echo that made it seem like we were in some unimaginably huge church. The nuns gasped in surprise. They would have clapped and cheered, but of course they couldn't do that at such a solemn moment. They did smile a lot, though, and tears ran down their cheeks.

At the end of the Mass, the bell started booming again. It rang until the chalice and the paten were washed, and the priest's vestments were put away.

Regent interrupted, "So somebody put a bell in the cupola as a Christmas gift to the nuns. That's nice."

"Let me continue," Liam said.

When I finished my duties in the sacristy and came back into the chapel – now your living room, as you know – I looked out and saw a crowd of people standing in the deep snow on the front lawn.

"We heard the bell," one of them explained to me. People were still coming up the hill, when the bell stopped.

No one knows why, but the people who came when the bell rang that Christmas Eve went about over the next twelve days making amends with those they had hurt or thought badly of during the previous year. People have been doing that in Oliver's Mountain ever since. Over time, observance of the Feast Day of St. John, the Apostle, the patron of love, honor, and friendship became a reminder.

Regent was stuck on the part of the story he could deal with rationally. He kept the part about the angels and doing annuals as far away as he could.

"Did anyone ever find out who had installed the bell?"

"That's the important part, Professor." Liam paused and smiled. "There was no bell. It did not exist until a year later, after the village had raised the money for one."

A frisson of uneasiness mixed with excitement washed over Regent. He did his best not to show it.

"Pardon me, Liam. You didn't find the bell. That doesn't mean it wasn't here. The same thing is happening now with the little replica bell you gave me."

Liam smiled still more broadly. "I was hoping you would see that. Well, I'll be going now."

Regent stood up to see his guest out and in doing so looked away for an instant. When he looked back, Liam was not there.

"Good night, Liam," Regent said under his breath.

Chapter Nineteen

Jane

Next morning, one of the village's two taxis turned into the driveway. Nurse led the way to it, while Scap stumbled along behind her scanning the newspaper classified ads as he went. Chandler had gone out earlier.

After they were gone, Regent told himself that he was happy to have the house to himself again. This was the way he liked it. All the commotion of recent days had been quite unnatural. Not his way. Not at all. And the solitude would make it easier to focus on planning his new life.

A warm climate seemed like a good idea. And a place where the cost of living was low. A dollop of high culture and a reasonably cultivated populace. Not that he planned to see anyone much. No, in this next chapter, he might get another dog and just enjoy being a private person again. Even insular. Nothing wrong with being insular.

He went to his computer and searched the web for retirement towns. Climate and affordability weren't hard to find. But in large measure, the descriptions were a combination of chamber-of-commerce wishful thinking and self-serving invention. And most important, all of these highly touted towns, even the smallest, were infected with sprawl.

This North Country village that he would soon be leaving, was blessedly different from most of America. It was mostly surrounded by dedicated parkland, so the sprouting of suburbs and malls was greatly inhibited. It had live theater and now and then performance of music that was neither rock nor country. He rarely went to plays or concerts, but he liked knowing they were there. A daily newspaper. It was thin on serious content, but there was one excellent columnist. Generally acceptable politics. He'd miss this place. He forced himself to think about something else before he got bogged down in regrets.

Dog breeds were covered in great detail on the web. There were pages and pages on every type of pooch known to man. Want to know how the Great Pyrenees came to be? It was there on the screen. Who breeds those winsome Labradoodles? It didn't matter, though; he didn't have nearly enough money to buy a purebred dog. Nonetheless, he was happily reading about Newfoundland Retrievers, when the doorbell rang.

He ignored it through several repetitions, then thoroughly annoyed, went to see who it was.

The caller had turned away and was starting to leave.

"May I ..." he started. His mouth fell open in surprise. He couldn't find words.

"Jane. Well. Uh... come in."

"Professor. Just give me a chance to explain."

Of all the things Regent felt, one was paramount: he was glad to see her. So glad, he opened his arms and embraced her. He didn't really do hugs, and she knew it. But he held her for a long moment.

"Welcome back, my dear." He also didn't address people as "dear."

At her feet was a new looking suitcase. She'd had a haircut, and her clothes were not those of a homeless person.

"It's sort of a long story," she started.

"In that case, you probably should take off your coat, and have a cup of coffee."

He didn't trust these feelings of kindness and understanding. After all, the manner of her leaving had been unacceptable, and her charity, however well-meaning, was humiliating. But he could be polite anyway.

"Thank you. But first..." Her voice trailed off as she pushed past him on the way to the kitchen. There she took the petty-cash box off the shelf and put some bills in it.

"That includes interest. I hope you all didn't think too badly of me. You probably did, though. I would have in your place."

They sat across from each other at the dining table. She'd only been gone a few days, but there was awkwardness between them as if it had been years, But Jane cut through it with her characteristic directness.

"You're looking good, Jane. That's a pretty sweater."

"Thank you." It hung in the air. "You made me very angry, Professor."

His impulse was to defend himself. *I didn't do one damned thing to make you angry.* But he just turned his head to one side in an expression of skeptical curiosity and waited for her to continue.

"I know quite a lot about getting grants." She waited for some affirmation from him.

"So you said."

"It was a big mistake for you to ask that North Country Charitable Trust to give you money with no strings attached. It will want to know specifically how you would use the grant. That's just how it works."

"I suppose you're right, but I would rather not have their support, if it means being regimented." He wanted to avoid arguing, but the pitch and volume of his voice rose as he added, "and it was *my* choice to make."

She stood up and almost yelled, "It was not *your* choice. Things have changed for you over the past week, and you haven't seen it. When you were here alone in this old house, choices were yours alone. But now, Nurse and Scap get a vote. And in some way yet to be determined, Dick is a participant. Sister Julia, too. You've even got me to deal with. Sure, it's your name on the mortgage, but we are all investors.

"Your dream of a creative community has become something we believe in. If you walk away from it, you are letting us down. We are part of your life now, and you better get used to it."

She caught her breath and sipped coffee.

Regent sighed deeply and changed the subject.

"OK. You were angry. Where'd you go?"

"To Connecticut. To see my uncle. He's my only living relative, and we've been estranged since my mother died. He's always been very disapproving of what he calls my bohemian ways – the term should tell you how retro he is. He thinks that being a writer is sort of disreputable. He has no children of his own, and he desperately wanted me to go into the family business."

"What kind of business?"

"Real estate – office buildings and commercial property. If you need 100,000 square feet of life-destroying office cubicles in Atlanta or San Francisco or almost anywhere in the world, he's your man."

"Well, how did it go with Uncle? From the look of things, pretty well."

"Miraculously well." She stopped and thought a moment before continuing.

"That evening after we'd all been talking about the grant application, I had a very strange experience. I had an urge to go see him. A really strong urge. It was as if I was compelled to go."

"Let me guess," Regent said. His anger had come to the surface. "You thought if you talked nice to your rich uncle, he would save poor old Dr. Regent's bacon."

"Back off, Professor," she shouted. "It was nothing like that." Her annoyance passed as suddenly as it had arrived. "No, no, it was, well, I hadn't had any contact with him for a long time, and I suddenly felt that I had to make things right with him as quickly as possible. I mean immediately. That's why I borrowed the grocery money and took off in the middle of the night."

"You could have left a note."

"I should have, but I was racing to catch the bus. And besides that, for a while there, I was, uh, not myself."

"So, did Uncle still want you to join the business?"

"Oh sure. I expect he'll always want that. But not like before. He's had a stroke, and he's a little disabled physically, but in another way, he's changed for the better. Before the stroke, everything was simple and absolute with him. He's still a bully and an oaf, but it seems like he may have developed some tiny capacity for recognizing complexity. That makes it easier to accept the 95% of him that's still abominable.

"And for the first time since I can remember, I'm able to feel something other than hostility toward him. Don't know where it came from." She shook her head slowly and frowned in thought.

"What did you say to him?"

"I said I was sorry that the choices I've made and the way I've lived have caused him pain. I don't have to point out to you, Professor Regent," she said with a grin, "that putting it like that is quite different from saying I was generally sorry for the choices I've made. And I asked him if there was anything I could do – other than go to work for him – to make things better between us."

"What did he say?"

She opened her eyes as wide as possible. "This part is amazing. It turns out that saying I was sorry was almost all he wanted from me."

Somewhat fearfully, Regent asked, "But you're still not going to work for him?"

"Of course not." She was back to shouting. "Listen to me, Professor. For such an intelligent person, you can be awfully slow to catch on. Listen to me. What I'm going to do is help you build Franklin Manor III, and I'm going to live here, and I'm going to write." She took a three-beat pause, then deadpanned quietly, "And, I'm going to take a little time now and then to save you from yourself."

He shook his head back and forth while she spoke. "Now, you listen, Jane. Your plans aren't going to work. The lender is going to take back the house. Nurse and Scap are out looking at apartments right now."

The color drained from her face. "You're giving up?"

"I wouldn't put it that way. It's more like what you did in not going into the family business. I'm being who I am."

"I don't get it. How does not making an effort to hold onto this house and your dream constitute being who you are?"

"You know the answer to that."

"I certainly do not, but it doesn't matter. I'm not going to let you do this. Not without you putting up a fight." She left the room angrily, the same way she had when they'd disagreed about the grant application.

Regent shrugged and got more coffee. A fine, wind-driven snow sprinted horizontally across the ground-level view from the kitchen window.

Chapter Twenty
Offers and What If's

Nurse and Scap shook the snow off their hats and coat out on the porch, then hung them in the mudroom.

"Hey, Professor, where are you?" Scap shouted.

Regent hesitated before answering. They might try to persuade him to reconsider his actions or they might be upset or the encounter might be unpleasant in some other way. He thought about feigning sleep.

Finally, he called out, "Upstairs. In my bedroom."

"Hey, it's really snowing out there," Scap said.

"Uh huh."

Nurse went over to the window and looked out at the village and across the frozen lake to Oliver's Mountain. The crusty white of old snow was turning to soft new white. "You're going to miss this view, Professor."

"I'll manage."

"Looking out this window must give you a lot of perspective."

"Uh huh." She was right, of course, but he wasn't going to encourage her.

"Are you still sure about giving up the house? Scap asked.

"Absolutely sure," he said. That was a little overstated, but in the circumstance, less certainty would not serve.

"I'm not sure I believe that," Nurse said, "but – "

"Believe it," Regent interrupted. His tone was sharp. He didn't want to argue the point. "Let's go down to the parlor."

He put more wood on the fire and poked it into life.

"We have a proposition for you," Nurse said.

Scap corrected her. "Not a proposition, a plan for a new life. One you will follow." He emphasized "will" and looked at Regent from under his brows, his chin tucked down in a posture that said, "I am serious."

What now? Regent thought.

Jane appeared in the doorway. "I thought I heard voices."

"Well look what the cat dragged in. The prodigal daughter," Scap said.

"Hello, Jane dear," Nurse said. She motioned Jane over to where she sat by the window and took her hand.

"As soon as we get through straightening out the Professor, I'll go kill a fatted calf," Scap said.

"Yes, let's tend to business first," Nurse said. "Professor, we've found an affordable apartment."

"Actually, it's a house," Scap said.

"Oh no," Jane groaned.

"Hold on, Jane," Scap said.

Nurse continued, "We've found an affordable house to rent, and it's large enough for all of us…" She gave Scap a questioning glance, and he nodded. "Including you, Jane."

Regent half closed his eyes and shook his head.

Scap said, "Don't even think about saying no, Professor. You haven't been making much sense the last couple of days, so just follow our lead on this."

He responded with a little grunt that could have meant anything.

Nurse continued. "There are enough bedrooms to allow us each to have our own. Including Dick, if he wants. Jane, you should be able to work quite handily in yours. We'll provide you a grant-in-aid – room and board – until you publish something profitable. The rest of us will pool our money to make expenses."

They all went quiet for a moment. Jane was the first to recover.

"I don't get it. You must think I robbed you, so how can you be so generous to me?"

Nurse and Scap looked at each other questioningly. Both looked at Regent. It didn't seem like the right time to tell her they knew about Uncle Ron's gift.

* * *

Regent would have spent the afternoon snowshoeing again, if the wind hadn't come up and dropped the chill factor lower than he liked. Instead, he stayed in his room, drank tea, tried unsuccessfully to read, then fell into what he knew he'd done too much of lately – brooding.

When they gathered for drinks, he went right to the point.

"You two are very kind to include me in your house plans, but I must decline."

"You get a better offer?" Scap teased.

"I've thought for some time now about leaving all this snow and cold weather behind." Actually, he'd only been thinking about it for a few hours, but that didn't matter. "So, Florida, here I come."

"Oh wow. I can just see that," Jane said. "Dr. Butch Regent, retired professor of English, playing canasta in a condo full of blue-haired widows and going to the dog races. You'd last about one day."

"When are you going?" Scap asked.

"Not until the foreclosure is completed, and I expect that'll probably take a few months."

"Good," Scap said. "That'll give us time to talk some sense into you. Right, Nurse?"

She smiled agreement, but she didn't look sanguine about the possibility.

Jane sighed deeply, stood up, and took a position with her back to the fire. She lacked only a white board and a marker for what came next.

"OK. here's what we're going to do now. Don't fight me on this, Professor. We're going to do a little what-if exercise. OK?"

She waited until he mumbled agreement.

"First, some background. For a little while you had a plan. Dick saw your letter to the bank asking for more time, remember, so we all know about it. Where is Dick, by the way?"

"Who knows?" Regent answered.

"Anyway, that was a persuasive plan you offered the lender, Professor. So, let's do what-if. What if the lender accepts it, and what if you do as you told them you would and look for a teaching job?"

Regent tried to interrupt.

"Let me finish. While you look, we pool our money. Nurse and Scap and you, Professor, put in your social security to meet ordinary expenses."

He tried again to interrupt. She talked over him. "And I'll do my part. I've already made an application for substitute teaching, and I was assured that I'd have more of it than I want."

"You did what? Jane, you've spent years refusing to work for wages so that you could pursue your writing. And now suddenly you're going to take a job and write part-time? Not just any job, either, but one that's frustrating, absorbing, distracting, and pays little. You can't do that."

"Yeah? You watch."

"You are being perverse."

"Then what if – "

Regent interrupted. "I know I should be saying thank you instead of being angry, but I don't feel grateful."

"You misunderstand, Professor. I'm doing this for me as much as for you. Now one more what-if. What if we redo the grant application?" Then she added, "properly this time. And what if we are successful, we catch up the payments, we make the mortgage lender happy, and we live happily ever after."

Nurse and Scap both looked at the floor. Regent and Jane locked eyes.

"You can stop with this, Jane. We know," Regent said.

"You know what? Oh, there's Dick."

Chandler shook the snow off his coat and hat and dropped them on the floor by the door.

"Jane. You're back."

"Hello, Dick. We were just getting to something important, so hold on a minute."

"I bet I know what it is."

"Make a drink or something, Dick. Let us finish this."

"No problem with making a drink, but maybe y'all would like to hear what Jane's uncle had to say to me?"

She shook her head like a dog coming out of water. "You've been talking to Uncle Ron?"

"It was not easy to get through to him – he has layers of protection to keep off casual callers. But when I finally did, we had a nice chat."

"What?"

"You should pay attention, now Professor. Uncle Ron says Jane has no knowledge of his payments to the lender."

"Oh sure." Regent's tone was as sarcastic as he could make it.

"I'm lost," Jane said. "What payments?"

"Oh stop, Jane. You know." Regent said.

"What are you talking about?" she said.

"This conversation is not going well at all," Nurse said. "Let me try to make it better. Jane, someone paid the arrears in the professor's mortgage. Dick investigated and learned that it was your Uncle Ron."

"Oh my God." she shouted. Regent could see that she was genuinely surprised.

"Professor – all of us, actually – assumed that you asked him to do it."

Dick said, "Not according to Uncle Ron. He's adamant that it was all *his* idea. Jane had mentioned this house and the Yaddo plan to him, but that was all. He got some of his minions to look into it, learned of the problem with the mortgage, and took it from there."

"That sounds just like him," Jane said angrily. "What a jerk that man can be."

Scap burst out laughing, and Nurse soon joined in.

"Is something funny?" Jane asked, her face turning red.

"You and Professor are," Scap answered. "Very funny. You're both as angry as you can be because someone has done you a favor."

The volume in Jane's voice rose again to shout level. "You don't understand. It's a control mechanism. For years Uncle Ron refused even to speak to me because I wouldn't go into his real estate business. A few days ago, I thought he had turned loose of that cockamamie idea. It seemed like he was finally willing to let me be myself. But no. Not him. He's got to stick his nose and his checkbook into my life, and make sure that I don't have any problems making my way."

Then she stopped talking. It was as if she'd listened to herself and heard something quite foolish. Scap and Nurse were still chuckling, and after a moment Jane began to laugh along with them. It caught hold of her and wouldn't turn loose for some time.

In the middle of it, she managed with some difficulty to say, "What do you say, Professor? Uncle Ron is hugely wealthy. A few thousand dollars are lunch money to him. Can we accept this gift?"

Regent grinned and said, "I'm a little ahead of you. While you all were being hysterical, I was thinking that when we get Franklin Manor III up and running, your Uncle Ron might want to come spend some time here. There's plenty of room. See what he helped build."

Regent fell into unrestrained laughing himself, and the others started again.

When calm finally returned and they wiped their eyes and were making little afterglow sounds that threatened to launch them into another fit, Nurse suddenly said, "Look." She pointed to the big bow window that opened onto the porch.

Tom was peering in, moving his head slowly back and forth, the bell hanging from his neck making a small tinkling sound.

When Regent went out on the porch, he found only tracks.

Chapter Twenty-One
Invitations

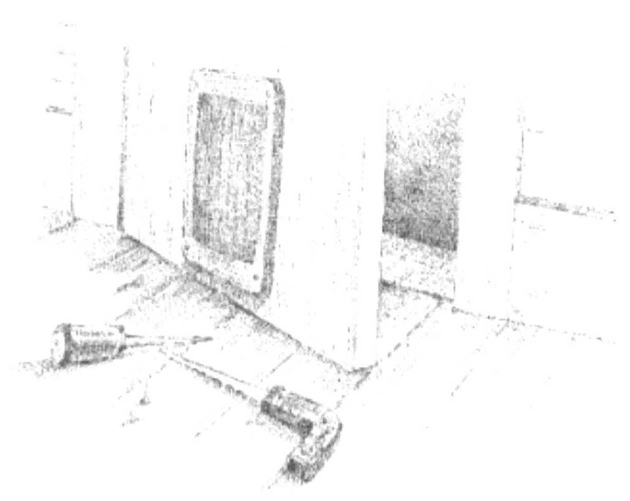

The bank readily agreed to disregard Regent's plan of deliberate default.

It was only slightly more difficult to come to agreement on how to word the grant application. Jane remained more pragmatic than Regent, but with some effort, plus some suggestions from Nurse, they managed in the end to write an application that suited them both.

When Chandler returned from the professor's study, where he'd been typing it, Jane said, "Dick, we've been talking about who is going to live here after we get the operating funds. And we were wondering what your plans are."

"Is that an invitation to join you? Could I really do that?"

"Sure," Regent said. "I thought you would have assumed that."

"I certainly have not. I'm quite flattered really. I'll stay at least until I get my story about the village finished. After that, I'll probably move along. You know, hunt where the ducks are."

"How's the story going?" Regent said. "Haven't heard you say much about it lately."

"Glad you asked, glad you asked. Coming together very nicely. It's got every element you could ever hope for in a story – drama, mystery, atmosphere. The focal point is the unique practice of doing annuals in the days following Christmas. So far as I know, that doesn't happen anywhere else. And the amazing disappearing cat. Your story about the bell and the Christmas dinner."

Regent looked around at the others. Their faces showed the same uneasiness he was feeling.

"I'm sure there are rational explanations for those things," Regent said. "And not to discourage you, Dick, but once the rational explanations are seen, the village is not all that interesting."

"You're right about that. Rational explanations would make it just another village. So, I'm going to take my time and do research until I'm sure these mysteries can't be explained away. Hey, I need some air. Why don't you sign the application, Professor, and I'll walk it over to Mr. Butcher's office."

As soon as the door shut behind Chandler, Scap said, "I don't like the sound of that. Never have liked the idea of publicity."

"Nor I," said Regent. "Such a story would destroy the village."

The others nodded agreement.

"I can see it now," Jane said. "The streets will be clogged with tour buses full of people come to see the quaint locals making rounds during the Twelve Days of Christmas. The exhaust fumes alone would turn the desire to make amends into anger and hostility."

Scap added, "Yes, and no cat in town will be safe. People will come from everywhere to try to catch the magical cat."

Nurse said, "Somebody'll probably start doing one of those *Son et Lumiere* shows like they have in Europe."

"I wonder if he's lined up a publisher yet?" Regent asked.

Jane said, "He told me he was going to write the story first, and then try to sell it."

"Where has he published before, Jane? Do you know?"

"No, I don't, but hold on a minute. I'll go see what I can find out."

Regent thought about whether the grant was going to be large enough so that he could buy another computer. It would be nice if he had a computer that was his alone the way he used to.

Jane was back a half hour later.

"I can't find a single reference to him. Not on Google, not anywhere."

Regent said, "That's odd. I got the impression he was a journeyman free-lancer. On the other hand, getting an assignment in a dream is not exactly standard operating procedure."

"I'm going to do something I shouldn't," Jane said. "I'll be back in a few minutes." She hurried up the stairs again.

Upon returning, she said, "I don't think we need to worry about Dick publishing this story. Chances are he will never finish it.

"I called a Tennessee phone number that I found in his bedroom. It turned out to be a halfway house for mental patients. Dick has been living there for some time. The story is that he does fine as long as he stays on his medication, but every time he leaves the facility and attempts to live independently, he stops taking it and relapses."

"He seems OK to me," Regent said. "Odd, but sane."

"Yes, he does, but according to the people I talked with, he should be just about out of his prescription. When that happens, we should expect the worst."

"Well, then we must get him a refill," Nurse said. "That shouldn't be difficult."

Scap nodded agreement. "Sure. We just invite Doc Scott over for a drink and tell him the situation. But why does taking his medicine mean he's not going to write the story?"

"It's not guaranteed," Jane said. "But it seems very likely. I was told that for years he's had the illusion that he's a writer. He's scribbled on Big Chief tablets and made plot notes and told people he's working on this and that and so on. Not very different from what I myself and countless others have done" – she paused and rolled her eyes – "do. But in his case, there is even more pretend in it than for the rest of us. His pattern has been to draft a short piece that's promising and never be able to write 'The End,' just can't stop revising and fiddling around. Too much risk or something.

"So, it seems to me he's not likely to finish this story about the village, either. He's never finished a story. He just writes and writes and never gets there."

"Poor man," Nurse said. "I wonder how we can help him."

They sat quietly for a few minutes, each of them trying to come up with something.

"OK, here's what we're going to do." Regent said, showing uncharacteristic self-assurance. "It's simple really. We'll persuade him to stay on with us here as a charter resident of Franklin Manor III. We invite Dr. Scott for cocktails regularly. Make him our team physician. What do you think, Scap? Will Scott do that?"

Nurse answered. "Sure he will. Scap and I have known him for years. He'll be happy to join us in this, and it will be good to have him."

"Great," Regent said. "As for the story, I'll just do what I can to keep Chandler looking for rational explanations for the mysteries he's observed. That'll keep him busy for a long time. We hope that he never finishes the story on the village, but – "

Jane took it from there. "I can help the poor guy with writing them. I'll be his coach. I'll give him exercises – coincidentally involving topics other than the mysteries of Oliver's Mountain – and we can read our material to each other – "

"Wait a minute," Regent interrupted. "I'm going to expect both of you to read your material to the rest of us whenever you have something ready. It's the sort of thing I've envisioned from the beginning."

"Yeah," Scap said, "And until Dick has something of his own to read, he can keep giving us 'Dangerous Dan McGrew.'"

They were still planning and talking about Chandler's future when he returned.

Regent said, "Dick, we've been thinking. We really don't want you to go. We're doing some planning, and we want to put you on the schedule for reading from your work in progress." He went on that way for a time.

When he paused for a breath, Chandler said, "Sure, why not? I like it here. Y'all are good company."

They talked a while longer, then Nurse called them to a dinner she thought might appeal especially to Dick – pork chops, turnip greens, and sweet potatoes.

"I wish I had known you were making this," Dick said. "The last place I lived I always made the cornbread. I'm good at black-eyed peas, too. Next time, y'all want some down-home food, let me help."

"We'll do that, Dick. We surely will," Regent said.

After an hour or so of television, everyone but Regent turned in. He had one more thing to do before going to bed himself.

He found his toolbox and went to a small, little-used basement door that was at ground level. He got down on his knees, drilled a hole, and inserted a keyhole saw. After a time, he leaned back and looked at the square opening he'd made.

One of these days I'll install a proper cat flap.

END

Don't miss out!

Visit the website below and you can sign up to receive emails whenever PAUL WILLCOTT publishes a new book. There's no charge and no obligation.

https://books2read.com/r/B-A-UYZS-AVWAC

BOOKS 2 READ

Connecting independent readers to independent writers.

Did you love *A Franklin Manor Epiphany*? Then you should read *A Franklin Manor Christmas*[1] by PAUL WILLCOTT!

A Franklin
Manor
Christmas

Paul WIllcott

Annals of Franklin Manor
. Book One[2]

For most potential buyers, Franklin Manor was just a huge run-down old house, a former monastery and tuberculosis sanatorium, half buried in Adirondack snow. But to erstwhile professor, Butch Regent, Franklin Manor was a beacon of hope. It would make his bland and unsatisfactory life meaningful. He would buy it, renovate it, and turn it into an artists' retreat. Lack of money, broken pipes, and pitiless cold almost defeat him but for the help of former patients, angels, a growing group of "temporary" guests, a long-dead altar boy, and a mysterious bell. In the end, the arists' retreat is beginning to take shape – but not in a way Regent recognizes.

---

1. https://books2read.com/u/4D68nk

2. https://books2read.com/u/4D68nk

It's a deep snow, feel-good story in the tradition of *Miracle on Fifth Avenue* and *The Bishop's Wife.*

Read more at paulwillcott.com.

Also by PAUL WILLCOTT

Annals of Franklin Manor
A Franklin Manor Christmas
A Franklin Manor Epiphany

Standalone
12,000 Miles of Road Thoughts. Old Van, Old Man, Recovering
Hippie, Dying Cat

Watch for more at paulwillcott.com.

About the Author

Paul Willcott is a lapsed Texan with four degrees from the University of Texas, including a Ph.D. in applied linguistics and a law degree. He is a veteran magazine writer, editor, publisher, award-winning newspaper columnist and blogger, novelist, and one-poem poet.

He has lived in Baghdad, Amman, Tehran, London, Hong Kong, Zurich, Washington, D.C., New York City, Saranac Lake, New York, and elsewhere. For many years, he and his wife Ann Laemmle lived in a former tuberculosis sanatorium/monastery in the Adirondack Mountains. They now live in New York City, where they feel more at home than anyplace they have lived.

Read more at paulwillcott.com.